## S. G. LEHRER

# The Crooner and The Comic

### The Story of Dean Martin and Jerry Lewis

First published by Kindle Direct Publishing 2020

Copyright © 2020 by S. G. Lehrer

All rights reserved. No part of this publication may be reproduced, stored or transmitted in any form or by any means, electronic, mechanical, photocopying, recording, scanning, or otherwise without written permission from the publisher. It is illegal to copy this book, post it to a website, or distribute it by any other means without permission.

First edition

Cover art by S. G. Lehrer

This book was professionally typeset on Reedsy.
Find out more at reedsy.com

*To my dad,*
*Who loves me always and forever, no matter what. He doesn't
believe me, but I love him more.*

# Contents

| | |
|---|---|
| *Foreword* | iii |
| *Preface* | v |
| Chapter One | 1 |
| Chapter Two | 9 |
| Chapter Three | 22 |
| Chapter Four | 25 |
| Chapter Five | 30 |
| Chapter Six | 38 |
| Chapter Seven | 42 |
| Chapter Eight | 48 |
| Chapter Nine | 52 |
| Chapter Ten | 61 |
| Chapter Eleven | 66 |
| Chapter Twelve | 70 |
| Chapter Thirteen | 75 |
| Chapter Fourteen | 79 |
| Chapter Fifteen | 83 |
| Chapter Sixteen | 91 |
| Chapter Seventeen | 96 |
| Chapter Eighteen | 102 |
| Chapter Nineteen | 109 |
| Chapter Twenty | 115 |
| Chapter Twenty-One | 122 |
| Chapter Twenty-Two | 127 |

| | |
|---|---|
| Chapter Twenty-Three | 133 |
| Chapter Twenty-Four | 139 |
| Chapter Twenty-Five | 145 |
| Chapter Twenty-Six | 150 |
| Chapter Twenty-Seven | 154 |
| Chapter Twenty-Eight | 159 |
| Chapter Twenty-Nine | 163 |
| Chapter Thirty | 167 |
| Chapter Thirty-One | 172 |
| Chapter Thirty-Two | 176 |
| Chapter Thirty-Three | 186 |
| Chapter Thirty-Four | 192 |
| Chapter Thirty-Five | 197 |
| Chapter Thirty-Six | 203 |
| Chapter Thirty-Seven | 207 |
| Chapter Thirty-Eight | 213 |
| Chapter Thirty-Nine | 219 |
| Chapter Forty | 225 |
| Afterword | 228 |
|   Bibliography | 231 |

# *Foreword*

I love Dean Martin and Jerry Lewis with all of my heart, and hold the utmost respect for them as individuals and partners. With this being said, the very last thing I would like this book to do is bring any disrespect, slander, or humiliation to their names. In order to stop that from happening, I have taken great care to do as much research as is possible and incorporate that into each and every chapter.

My goal as a writer is to bring readers into a world; in this case, it is the world of Dean Martin and Jerry Lewis. In order for that to happen and not be distracted from, I have been careful to add as many phrases and references faithful to each time period as possible, but have refrained from including very many foreign words that would confuse the reader.

As a part of my research, I have read many terrific biographies of the two, but one aspect of them I did not like were the books' crassness. To be faithful to who Dean and Jerry were, I was not afraid to include a certain extent of unkind words and references to promiscuity outside the confines of marriage and whatnot, but so that a wider audience can hear and experience their journey, I have limited those vulgarities to only what is absolutely necessary.

For those of you who have read autobiographies, biographies, and other source material related to the two, you might find similarities in dialogue or description in certain scenes—perhaps even complete replicas! That is because I find that when dialogue has already been set out explicitly from someone with insider knowledge, or an experience has been described by the very person who felt it firsthand, that is the best and most accurate the description is going to get. After all, the purpose of my book is to create the most holistically accurate biographical novel as to how Jerry and Dean experienced life together and apart, so I believe that in certain instances using verbatim accounts told by other authors would aid that purpose.

As a final note, I recognize that both Dean's life and Jerry's life was multifaceted, and revolved around their wives, their work, their hobbies, their children, and each other. But for the sake of being concise, and since the book's focus is on their partnership, I could not include everything, but did my best to choose wisely what to include and what to leave out.

# Preface

Although this book is primarily aimed at readers who are already familiar with and savor the partnership of Dean Martin and Jerry Lewis, I recognize that there are always going to be readers who fall outside of the generalized category. So, I wanted to include a brief history of who they are.

From 1946—1956, one comedy duo reigned high above almost all other comedians, singers, actors, and actresses in a fashion similar to 'Beatlemania'. Their names were Dean Martin and Jerry Lewis, but were known to the public simply as 'Martin and Lewis'. They had an immediate, unbelievable rise to fame in 1946, working primarily in nightclubs. The essence of their act is what they were commonly referred to as: sex and slapstick. Dean Martin represented sexuality, and Jerry was uninhibited, chaotic, slapstick. They became the hottest thing in the country, and soon had a deal with Paramount to make movies. They made a total of sixteen movies throughout their 10-year career, had several tries at a radio show for NBC, and had done over a dozen shows for the Colgate Comedy Hour. They had a fantastic career together, and when they split in 1956— for reasons still debated today—they ended up having fantastic individual careers.

But what set them apart wasn't their accomplishments. It was their true, genuine love for each other, and their breaking the barriers of comedy as it was at the time. You see, with Bing Crosby and Bob Hope, they had a certain chemistry, but no one was under any impression that they *loved* each other. With Dean and Jerry, it was so apparent that they truly and genuinely cared for each other. They played entirely to each other—in many instances it was as if the audience didn't exist. They were having fun onstage together, and the audience could tell. They were like family, and they weren't afraid to show it.

Now, as an act, they brought something new to the stage. Before them were Stan Laurel and Oliver Hardy. Those two represented simpler times when all you needed was an unexpected hit on the head or someone to trip to get a good laugh. As a duo, Stan represented the simpleton—almost a child, but not quite. Unassuming, but clumsy and a bit slow in the mind. Oliver was the high-class; the exasperated sophisticate who would look to the audience knowingly after yet another of Stan's messes. Martin and Lewis weren't entirely of a different cloth, they were just a different shade. They were younger, and more vibrant. There was slapstick, but there was also comedy just in who they were. Unlike Stan, Jerry *was* a child! He was the completely uninhibited manchild with no self-control; he'd holler and be completely overcome around a pretty girl, he'd cry and have a tantrum when things went awry, and he'd show his affection for Dean in the most unfashionable of ways. Unlike in the relationship between Laurel and Hardy, Dean was always the paternal chum of Jerry; the one who looked out for him and kept him safe—and the audience safe from Jerry. As for Dean himself, he was everything Oliver was, but with sex appeal. Their act was fresh, and it was simply what the world needed at that point in time.

That's why I've written this book: to show the world these two men who transformed comedy and what love looks like. I hope you come away from this book with a greater understanding of what they've brought to the world—and I hope you fall in love with them like I have.

# Chapter One

Name: Joseph Levitch (Jerry Lewis)

Year: 1932

Age: 6

Mom's gone again . . . Dad hasn't been here for days . . . and I'm all alone. I shoot up from the kitchen table, flinching as the screeching of the chair against the tile breaks the deafening silence. I stand stock still in the middle of the dimly lit kitchen, blood pounding in my ears, until a torrent of emotions abruptly washes over me, and my legs begin moving. My bare feet pound against the cold tile and then the hardwood floors of the hallway as I run out of the apartment and into the frigid night air.

The surprising colors of bright yellow and orange surrounding me like a cloud as they hang above me on trees and fall to the sidewalk are almost beautiful...they probably would have been if it weren't for the terrifying, indescribable panic that keeps my feet moving.

"Mommy..." I sob as I hurry past dishevelled men sprawled in the street, sleeping off more whiskey than they could afford, and stray men and women walking to a late night cocktail party. Any one of them could have been President Hoover for all I care; I can only think about the mounting fear that I would never see Mommy again. I'm alone, and I'm scared.

As I turn the corner, an offensive brightness cuts through the tears blurring my vision, and the familiar, sweet, sweet sound of the piano that my mom always plays makes me cut into the bar to my left. The hope that swells within me is almost overtaken by the raucous laughing, overwhelming reek of cigar smoke, and the feeling of being small and lost. But when I glimpse her slender fingers moving across the keys like they're creatures independent of her control, I cry out and maneuver between the tables until I am gazing up at her with glassy eyes and a trembling lower lip.

When she finally sees me, a yelp escapes her lips, and she grabs my hand hurriedly to lead me out of the bar. She stops only to tell an angry—looking man in a tweed suit where she's going, and then we are out in the biting wind again. She is walking so quickly, and her grip on my hand so tight, that I have to run to keep up.

Finally mom comes to a halt, and I hear her sob.

"Don't cry, mommy, please! I didn't mean anything, I didn't know where you went! I was all by myself! Please, mommy!" I cry out in panic, tugging on her hand so she would turn to look at me. I don't want her to be mad.

## Chapter One

"Oh, Joey, I'm sorry." Mom turns around to face me with eyes glistening, and she kneels down to wrap her arms around me in a momentary embrace. She kisses my forehead tenderly, and I close my eyes for what feels like an eternity. She loves me. She truly cares for me. What a wonderful feeling.

**6 Months Later**

"Honey, we've got to leave now or we won't be back in time for rehearsals!" Mom calls out cheerily, brushing her dark hair in the mirror as dad emerges from the bathroom in his swim trunks. I don't know why she tries to look so nice when she's only going to get all wet in a minute or so. I finish unpacking my clothes and putting them in the top drawer of the nightstand by the bed, and smile. This time unpacking my clothes doesn't mean I'm about to stay at Aunt Rose's or someone else's house. I'm with mom and dad now.

Finally we get around to leaving for the pool, and I can hardly keep from skipping through the halls, I'm just so excited. What a place! I feel like I'm in a dream as we pass the almost shockingly blue floors and stark red couches of the lobby, and I remember seeing the outside of the President's Hotel for the first time, with it reaching so high and far that I felt like I was an ant, but at the same time I knew I wanted to live somewhere like that someday.

We end up going swimming for about an hour, and that's fun and all, but I just can't wait to see mom and dad in rehearsals—I think secretly they can't wait to be in rehearsals, either.

It turns out I was right when we show up at the stage they're going to be performing on tonight. Mom is practically glowing, and dad has that confident hint of a smile on his face I so rarely

## The Crooner and The Comic

see—I so rarely see him at all, come to think of it. They have me sit just off stage behind the curtains, and at first I'm sore about it because I wanted to see them perform like everyone else will get to tonight, but as I look around, I realize I can see the other performers practicing their routines.

Just in front of me is a line of girls with arms linked together, kicking their legs. Suddenly a man in a three button suit and a straw boater hat darts onto stage from behind me and invites himself into the line of girls. He begins dancing with them—badly—but everyone seems to be having a good time, and then he tries to do a leap into the air but falls on the ground, crushing his hat. I laugh, and when I look around, I see everyone else is too.

The man runs off the stage after an exaggerated bow, and I suddenly decide that's what I want to do. Some kids want to be policemen when they grow up. Others want to be firemen. But I want to make people laugh.

The last people to rehearse on stage are three male dancers in suits, with canes and boater hats like the man who had clowned around before. They begin to do some tap dancing, but then they keep stopping after half a minute, gesturing and saying things I can't hear to the band behind them. I sure hope it isn't what they're planning to do for the show, because it isn't very good.

"Joey? We've got to get going now. Daddy and I have to get ready for the show." Mom says from behind me, and I turn to face her from atop a barrel, with my feet dangling a foot or so from the ground.

"Can I stay, mommy? I want to see everyone until they're all done." I plead with her, a hopeful smile on my face. She turns to dad, whose normal composed appearance is missing, with

## Chapter One

a sheen of sweat over his face and his hair unruly. He stares at me sharply for a moment before shrugging and beginning to walk back to our room. I exhale in relief and kiss mom on the cheek before looking back at the men on stage.

To my surprise, they're gone, and the band is packing up their instruments. I hop off the barrel and turn around to look at the variety of things left behind in the backstage. Lots of spare clothes from the girl dancers, a few hats, and canes and such. I reach down to pick up a cane and almost drop it, having not anticipated it to be so heavy. When I stand it up all the way it's just about as tall as I am. With excitement flowing through me, I eagerly pick up a straw hat and plop it onto my head. It's way too big, of course, so I tip it backwards to be able to see anything.

Glancing around to make sure no one is watching, I walk over to the stage and face the theater. I feel like I'm home. I feel like I'm where I'm supposed to be. A smile crosses my face, and I start to stomp the ground the kind of way I saw some of the men doing. I end up losing my balance and tripping, causing the cane to fly out of my tiny hands, and I scowl before it occurs to me that the man earlier was tripped just like me, and everyone laughed. I do the same thing, except I try to slip this time in a more exaggerated way, and I look out at the empty theater wishing for an audience. This is just the beginning.

\* \* \*

### The Crooner and The Comic

Name: Joseph Levitch

Year: 1932

Age: 6

About half a dozen conversations are going on at once, some in English, some in Yiddish, all pleasant and light, wafting towards me through the air like the delightful smell of the Brisket coming from my plate. I don't pay too much attention to any particular conversation; I just kind of drift in and out of each one—the trivial, gossipy ones of my aunts or the boring ones coming from my uncles.

But abruptly I'm forced to tune into a particular one: Uncle—although he's my step grandpa, I always call him Uncle— shouts loud enough for everyone to glance up in dismay, "WHAT! You tell *me* I shouldn't drink what I want in my own house?" Then I watch in disbelief as he smacks Grandma across the face with the back of his hand. Her head whips to the side, and his expression remains nonplussed beneath his thick mustache.

It's only when he raises his hand to strike her a second time, causing Uncle Bernie to punch him square in the jaw, that all of the shock leaves me. It's replaced by molten anger ripping through me and sending me lunging across the table with a shriek I hardly recognize as my own: "I'll kill you!"

Somehow in my all-encompassing range I hurtle past the grasping hands of relatives and latch onto the back of Uncle's

## Chapter One

neck, acting as a dead weight against his neck. All I can think about is that he hit Grandma. He hurt Grandma. The only one in the world who cares for me. The only good thing in this world. I'll kill him. I'll kill him if I have to die trying.

I don't get the opportunity to follow through with my promise as hands stronger than my body, but not my will, pull me from Uncle.

\* \* \*

The bread knife fits perfectly in my hand; in the back of my mind I have the faint notion that it should be much heavier and much bigger, but then again, it's my dream, so I can make it how I want it. There he is. Uncle's slumped over at the table, only the overhead light from the kitchen cutting through the midnight darkness. I creep nearer and nearer to him, though I hardly need to be quiet given the state he's in.

Finally I'm so close to him I can smell the alcohol on his breath; it takes all the willpower I have not to gag. With heartbeat quickening, I grab a fistful of his sweaty hair in my free hand and lift his head from the table. His eyes remain closed, and I focus in on his exposed neck.

I hate you. Without a second's hesitation I slash the knife across his throat. Then the blood comes . . . so much blood.

"Grandma!" The cry is on my lips before my eyes fly open. Fear rolls through me, and when I don't see Grandma rushing through the dark into my room, I rip off the sheets and sprint to her room as if someone's chasing me. Standing by the side of her bed, I can't stop myself from trembling. "Grandma?" I whimper again, and I hear her sit up in bed.

"What is it?"

### The Crooner and The Comic

"A nightmare . . . " Her hands reach out in the dark, finding me and pulling me to her.

"I know, Sonny . . . I know."

# Chapter Two

Name: Dino Crocetti (Dean Martin)

Year: 1931

Age: 14

What the hell am I doing at this stupid school? I don't need to know who won what war, and when. I need to fight my own wars, and George Washington sure isn't going to help me win them.

The bell signaling the end of the day pulls me from my thoughts, and my face hardens in indignation as I sweep my books into one arm and leave the room along with the other students.

As I pass Barbara's desk, I notice her looking at me from the edges of my vision, and I toss her a playful grin. She smiles

## The Crooner and The Comic

back, looking up at me from beneath her long, blond lashes, and I continue on my way.

I only stop at my locker long enough to toss my books in, and I slam it closed a little harder than usual. I'm no five-year-old, I shouldn't still be doing this, listening to these stupid broads who've got nothing to *tell* me I need. There's a reason why they pay us to go to college, not the other way around. They couldn't pay me a million dollars to go to college.

Jogging down the stone steps of the entrance to the school, I blink against the harsh sunlight, and I make out a group playing aerial passes with a soccer ball. I don't plan on joining the game, but as I pass their area of the field, hands in my coat pockets, they call out to me to play. I shake my head, but they continue: "Come on, just one pass?!" Finally I sigh, unbutton my coat, and lay it folded on the edge of the field before abruptly breaking into a sprint.

A few of the boys run after me, but the rest are too caught off guard to follow. After about five seconds, though, the boys fall back, unable to catch up with me, and after a few more seconds of feeling the wind whip past my face, I turn towards the group, and the ball rockets towards me. Perfect. The leather stings my forearms as I catch it, but I catch it nonetheless. The boys break into cheers, and, panting, I drop the ball and stroll back to where my coat is. I pick it up and brush the grass off before carefully pulling it on and buttoning it up.

As I stroll away from the field, heart slowing to its normal pace again, a car pulls up beside me. Joan rolls down her window and pushes her long, dark curls from her piercing blue eyes.

"Good catch." She says softly.

"Thanks."

## Chapter Two

"Am I still seeing you tonight?"

"Wouldn't miss it for the world." I croon back, and am about to turn away from Joan when I realize she is still looking up at me hopefully; expecting something. I already told her I was coming tonight. With that thought, I walk away.

\* \* \*

"Hey, look, it's the sissy!" The call comes from the leader of a group of boys standing in the road blocking my way, a real greaseball senior who thinks he's better than everyone else.

"Lemme through, Eddie." I say shortly.

"Why should I?"

"Whaddya tryna do? Start a fight? If you are, I'm in the mood to boff someone. Particularly you." The words come out softly and slowly as I brazenly lock eyes with Eddie.

"Now why would I want to do that? I'm just havin' fun."

"Sure, pally." I cut through the group, and am almost in the clear when Eddie mumbles under his breath, "You sure wouldn't stand a chance if I did fight ya." Now, most days, I wouldn't give him a second glance, but today everyone seems to be asking for a shot in the mouth. So, that's exactly what I give him. Before they can blink, Eddie is clutching at his mouth as blood runs through his fingers. I straighten my sleeves and keep walking through the neighborhood towards my house.

"Ya didn't have to blow your wig, Dino, we were just kidding!" Someone shouts to me over the chaos that erupted, but I ignore him.

"I'm gonna get you for this, you damn daego!" Eddie shouts over the crowd. I turn the corner home with a satisfied smile.

### *The Crooner and The Comic*

## A Year Earlier

"That's too bad. Just a little bit off. Well, what can ya do?" I shrug, a mocking smile playing on my lips. Because Conrad was a few years older than me, he made the mistake of thinking he was better than me at pool. He was wrong. I've been playing pool since I could hold a cue stick.

I can tell he's getting nervous; Conrad has plucked his pocket square out and is now dabbing at his forehead with it, all while his eyes flit back and forth between the table and me. So naturally I decide to make a show of slowly circling the table, despite knowing exactly what I'm going to do next, making sure to push Conrad closer against the wall each time I pass.

Finally I stop and with one swift movement bend down and place the tip of the cue lightly against the ball. The pounding of my heart that had begun as I realized the stakes of this final shot ceases as my body moves almost on its own from doing this thousands of times. In this one moment everything else around me slips away, and I'm only aware of the bright glint of the light against the cue ball, and the cool, smooth wood of the cue stick between my fingers.

I can tell my strike against the ball is perfect as soon as it happens, and I step back with a grin as it knocks the final ball into the pocket. Conrad curses under his breath, and, fuming, slaps down a ten dollar bill on the edge of the table without meeting my eyes.

I am about to make a snide remark to him while reaching for my money when someone behind me places their hand on my shoulder. Stiffening, I nonetheless pocket the bill before turning around to face whoever it is. Not one, but three, boys varying in age between about 13 and 19 stand facing me, but

## Chapter Two

they don't seem sore at me for anything, so I lean back against the wall and take out a cigarette before saying, "Whadda you fellas want?" One of them, who looks about as old as me with a hooked nose and greased up black hair, whips out a lighter from his coat pocket. "Light?"

"Thanks." I say warily through the cigarette between my teeth as I lean down and light my cigarette.

"You did pretty good back there, kid." The oldest one says loudly with a scrutinizing expression, and I take a drag from the cigarette before responding in the same way, "Thanks, mack."

"I'm John," The oldest one says, pointing to himself, "This is Jiggs, and that's Mandy."

"I'm Dino. Did you have something else to tell me?"

"Yeah. You want to make some real money?"

\* \* \*

This was a mistake. Oh, God, I thought I could do this, but I don't think so. I stand in the middle of the sidewalk, frozen, as a cop car cruises past me. I can feel a tension, an anxiety mounting within me, but excitement begins to drown it out. What am I afraid of? I don't even have anything illegal on me yet! This is a chance to make some real dough, and I'm not going to mess that chance up by being . . . afraid. I'm too old for that.

I continue down the dimly lit street with a renewed vigor, softly whistling "Mari, Mari". I like it here at night. No people to pass on the sidewalks. No reek of car exhaust in the street. Just the darkness interrupted by the occasional street light, and the melancholy sound of "Mari, Mari" echoing through the night.

I hear the low rumble of its engine before I catch sight of the black Ford Coupe idling in the alley as I round the corner, lights off, just another shadow in the quiet night. As I approach the car, I make out the immediately recognizable silhouette of Slick sitting in the back, and I think Jiggs is in the driver's seat. Without hesitation, I jerk the passenger door open and slide into the car.

With an effort not to appear nervous, I slowly turn my head so I can see them out of the corner of my eye: it *is* Jiggs and Slick, and I exhale softly in relief. Jiggs is staring ahead with such intensity that I'm sure any person caught in the crosshairs would have just about withered, and Slick has a frown set beneath his dark beard, but I presume it's probably because of the crates that are almost crushing him to death.

Straightening, I smirk and say with a level, almost disinterested voice, "Why the glum faces, pallies? We're here to make money, aren't we? Let's get this show on the road." Jiggs breaks from his trance and nods, pressing his foot on the gas. Slick still looks just as uncomfortable, but what are you gonna do?

The ride into Canonsburg isn't too hard. A little long, and a little cold, perhaps. That is, until we reach our destination. We finally ease to a stop around the back of a bookstore, and as we unload the crates, the only things I know are that this ain't no regular bookstore, and those ain't no books.

"What are we delivering?"

"Books. Special books." He lets out a harsh laugh, but I can tell it's more out of nervousness than anything. As we reach the back door and knock, I lean over and whisper to him, "Why are you so jumpy? Haven't you done this before?"

"We're late." Is all he whispers back, and I square my

## Chapter Two

shoulders with an inaudible sigh. The door is suddenly jerked open from inside, and a dishevelled, rather round man sticks his head out, blinking as if he just woke up. "What is it?!" He barks, and Jiggs says calmly, "We have the special books you ordered."

"What order? It's three in the morning!" The man retorts, squinting at Jiggs suspiciously. I glance over to Jiggs, and see a flash of confusion cross his face. "The order. You know." He says it slowly this time, as if he's saying the sky is blue to a twit.

"No. I *don't* know, so get outta here before I call the coppers." My heart drops as I watch Jiggs' hand reach under his coat for a rod, and I instinctively shove my hand in my pocket, fingers curling around the cold grip of my switchblade.

We are abruptly saved from doing something stupid when the door swings completely open, and another man appears with a hardened expression on his face. "It's okay, Jimmy, I can take it from here." He says with a thick Italian accent, and the man glares at Jiggs for another second before grumbling under his breath and shuffling back into the building.

"You're late." The man says, holding up his right arm to reveal a gold wristwatch beneath his pinstriped suit sleeve.

"I know. It took longer than expected. It won't happen again."

"It won't. Now bring them inside." With that, the man turns on his heel and disappears inside the building.

We all sigh in relief as soon as the door slams shut behind him, and I turn to Jiggs as we all go back to unloading the boxes.

"Why didn't you tell me you were packing heat? I would have come prepared!"

"You should always come prepared, or you're gonna end up

in a Chicago overcoat."

\*\*\*

Name: Dino Crocetti

Year: 1932

Age: 15

"So, you're gonna be initiated tomorrow, huh?"
"That's right." I answer slowly, eyeing George warily. He's been through it, he knows what it's like . . . he's just *trying* to roil me up.
"You scared?"
"I don't know what the hell to be scared *of*! I've heard the stories, but I don't know what's true . . . come on, mac, tell me what to expect!" I flick away my cigarette in annoyance, and George's eyes glint mischievously.
"You know I can't tell you that, Dino . . . Just know that you'd better be willing to do anything for them. And I mean *anything . . .* "
I've tried counting sheep. I've even tried sleeping upside down in bed. But none of the tricks in the book work. I just can't stop thinking about tomorrow—what they're gonna do to me. What they could make me do.
My eyes burn as I gaze up at the ceiling, and I try to clear my mind. Just not think about anything whatsoever. The racing of my heart slows, and I close my eyes hopefully once more.

## Chapter Two

I wonder what to bring tomorrow as I turn on my pillow. I don't finish the thought.

\* \* \*

*It can't be that hard. I've seen people's fingers broken, one by one. I've seen the life leave someone's eyes as they're shot in the head, point blank.*

*Besides, I'm sure this guy deserves it. The organization doesn't order a hit unless they deserve it.*

"You ready, Dino?" Rick's whisper isn't urgent, but still edged with a hint of excitement as they stop in front of Cira's Jewelry Store. There's one flickering light over the entrance, casting a disconcerting orange-tinted glow a few feet in every direction

"Let's just get this over with." I mutter, managing to find my voice, and quickly move forward until my fingers are tightly curled around the door handle.

Taking a moment to slow the frenzied racing of my heart, I then pull the handle with trepidation. The man standing behind the counter, organizing a shelf of necklaces, looks the same as he did in the picture the gang showed me yesterday, only a little bit friendlier. As he realizes we're there and glances up at us, I see that he has a barely noticeable white Clark Gable moustache, and the corners of his clear eyes droop slightly.

"Can I help you boys?" The man asks in a wary tone, noting our ages.

"Yeah, actually. You've got something we want." I begin, proud that no nervousness slips through into my voice.

"What might that be?" There's a note of alarm in the man's voice, and he drops his arm to reach for something underneath the counter. It takes me a split-second to whip out my gun, having practiced

*The Crooner and The Comic*

*my fast draw a hundred times in the mirror to be like Tom Mix. The man raises his hands in defeat, only a twitch of a cheek muscle giving away his panic. "Alright boys, take all the jewelry you'd like, only don't think you're gonna get away with it!"*

*"We don't want your jewelry, Mister! We want the money you owe us!" Rick blurts out, and I can tell he's eager for a fight, so I shake my head once at him. Crossing his arms begrudgingly, Rick turns back to the man, who looks confused for several moments.*

*"Oh! You guys are Frankie's boys! Look, I told you, our sales haven't been too good lately, and I hardly have enough money to feed my family as it is!" I shove down the rising pang of sympathy, and my fingers tighten around the handle of the gun.*

*"Give us the money or you die." The next words that come out of the man's mouth honestly shock me so that my eyes widen.*

*"Ya can't get blood from a turnip. I got a hundred dollars in the till, and that's to put food on the table. If you're going to point that gun at me, you might as well use it, because I don't got nothin' to give you." The tiring wear of age on the man's face all but disappears as he stares brazenly at me with the determined expression of one who's ready to die.*

*"This is going to be easier than we thought it would. Do it, Dino!" Rick urges, a glint in his grey eyes that I find myself repulsed by. But nevertheless, I don't have a choice.* This is what I want. *I look back to the man, and raise the gun level with his head. My index finger slowly, steadily reaches out towards the trigger. The tip of my finger touches the metal, and a shiver runs down my spine.* This is what I want. *I force myself to look into the man's eyes, a light blue torched with anger, daring me—it's clear there's going to be no begging. A quick breath that catches in my throat.* This is what I want. *I pull the trigger, and my whole body reacts with the jerk of the gun, the deafening boom, the smell of gunpowder that fills my*

18

## Chapter Two

nostrils, and the man that drops to the ground a split second later.

I don't need Rick to pull me away, for everything sends me into motion and running away from the scene faster than I've ever run before. Rick and I don't stop until we're just out of town, leaning on a tree somewhere, catching our breath. Rick is laughing as soon as he takes in a few gasps of air, but my head spins dizzily.

I can't exactly put into words why I feel sick to my stomach. Why I was so hesitant to do what needed to be done. I should be laughing, right? That's what everyone else does. They don't give anyone else a second thought.

I let out a short, harsh laugh. I don't feel like laughing, though. I glance down at the gun in my hand, and feel a thrill run through me. I hold the power of life and death—and used it. I laugh again. This time it's real.

"Congratulations, Dino. You're one of us now."

An hour later it's time for my official initiation. I'm driven, blindfolded, across town and then am led inside what I think is a house, and down two flights of stairs until I'm stopped, and I hear the creak of a door opening. Smoke fills my lungs, and the blindfold is promptly ripped from my head.

I blink rapidly, and eventually see I'm in the doorway to a room that is in shadows except for a card table in the center that's illuminated by a single light bulb hanging precariously from the ceiling. All the biggest names of our branch of the mafia are sitting around the table, each armed with either a handgun or strapped with a more heavy duty weapon.

I realize I've been standing there, just looking at them, for a second too long when I'm pushed from behind into the only empty chair at the table. Someone steps out from the shadows and places a dagger and a pistol on the table in front of me, and my heart beat quickens as I wonder what else they're going to make me do—or do to me.

### *The Crooner and The Comic*

The don at the head of the table seemingly takes no notice of the weapons and instead motions for us all to stand. We do so, the scraping of chairs against the floor a relief from the silence. He has us say the rules we must all follow in Italian, though I understand them all to mean roughly these three things: "Be loyal to members of the organization. You must never betray your wife. You must never become involved with narcotics."

We all sit back down, and my heart is practically vibrating with the excitement of it all—finally I'm going to be part of the organization. The silver glint of a needle dims that excitement with fear, but only for a moment. The one next to me wordlessly takes my index finger and pricks it with the needle. Whispers of pain and pressure come as he squeezes until he deems enough blood has dropped onto the picture of a saint he holds out beneath it.

"This blood means that we are now one family. You live by the gun and the knife and you die by the gun and the knife." Like the man from the store? An image of the man's blood staining the glass of the display flashes through my mind, and I blink it away.

I nod, despite it all somewhat relieved that I don't have to do anything more grueling, but I am dismayed to be wrong as the man lights the blood-soaked picture on fire. Flames lick at one corner of the picture, and he hands it to me.

"Take it and pass it around." I don't dare disobey the order, though every instinct inside of me—and my fingers—scream for me not to. We all pass it along until it's no longer burning despite the sting, and I'm wowed by the grim expressionless faces, and finally the don says to me with a pointed look, "Do you swear that if you disobey the rules, your flesh will burn like this saint?"

I'm barely able to suppress a shudder at those words, and just slowly nod, lips pressed tightly together. "Say it."

"I swear," I begin, excitement and fear filtering through to my

## Chapter Two

voice, *"that if I disobey the rules, my flesh will burn like this saint."*

* * *

My eyes flicker open, and I sit up in bed. That was just a dream. That was just a dream?

**Later that Day**

"Well done, Dino. You're one of us, now."

"Thanks." I smile grimly as they file out of the room, each one patting me on the back or shaking my hand. Was it worth it?

# Chapter Three

Name: Joseph Levitch

Year: 1935

Age: 9

I would rather be anywhere than here. I shut my eyes tightly for a moment, willing this to be just some sort of demented nightmare, but when they flicker open I'm still in an empty classroom.

"Alright everyone, come in and line up against the blackboard as I tell you all which seat is yours!" Mrs. Davis calls out with a gap-toothed smile, waving to the group waiting just outside the room, and I slouch in my chair slightly with eyes downcast. I can tell by the footsteps ringing throughout the room that they have begun to shuffle inside one by one.

*Chapter Three*

I can already feel their eyes boring into the back of my head, and I bite my lip. I don't want them to think I'm ashamed or that I've done something wrong . . . I *am* older than them. So, I take a deep, quivering breath and straighten in my seat, meeting their eyes boldly. As they line up against the blackboard, some of them seem to be even more nervous than I am, and avoid my gaze. Others stare at me curiously, whispering to their friends why they think I'm sitting there.

"I know him. He's a year older than us."

"What is he doing here, then?"

"I think he was held back."

"Wow, you have to be pretty dumb to be held back."

My eyes sting as tears fill my eyes, and my cheeks burn with embarrassment. I'm not dumb. I just couldn't catch up with the work because I was moving all the time! I think . . .

Finally they're all inside, and Mrs. Davis has stopped them all from talking, but things aren't over yet. She still has to tell them all which seats are theirs. One by one.

\* \* \*

Name: Joseph Levitch

Year: 1937

Age: 11

"Come on, Joey, she wants to meet you." Dad urges me, a glint of something I can't quite place in his dark eyes. He

## The Crooner and The Comic

motions for this lady in a dancing uniform to come over, and she struts towards us, her heels clicking against the wood floor rhythmically.

"Say hello to Marlene, son." I look up shyly at her, and she smiles broadly back at me, dimples appearing on both of her pink cheeks. She's very pretty, with long, dark eyelashes framing eyes just a hint greener than mine, and light brown hair curled around her heart-shaped face.

"H—hi." I eventually manage, my mouth dry and palms sweaty.

"Don't be shy, sweetie, I won't bite you!" She says in a sing-songy voice, giggling at the end. I can't say anything else, so I just smile at her, trying to slow the racing of my heart.

A night later, Marlene takes me into her dressing room and shows me she was telling the truth. It was wonderful and terrifying at the same time. I didn't understand what it was all about and I didn't know how to feel. I was excited and ashamed. I felt like an adult and I felt like I wanted to hide. For some reason, afterward she suddenly bursts into tears and starts saying things about her son. I don't understand any of it, but her red-rimmed eyes and trembling lips prove too much for me, and I slip out of the room under the meek excuse of having to go to bed.

## Chapter Four

Name: Dino Crocetti

Year: 1936

Age: 19

Clink. God, I hope no one heard that. I move my foot as slowly as I can within my oversized loafers to move the silver dollar out of the way and underneath my foot. Once it slides beneath my heel, I sigh inaudibly, the cool surface of the coin for a moment taking away the dull ache of having to stand for hours on end.

As I palm a stack of silver dollars and slide it over to one of the players sitting across from me with his hat blocking the light from hitting his face, my large hand easily covers the one I hold onto.

*The Crooner and The Comic*

Once their attention is all diverted back to their cards, I drop my hand behind the table, angling it before letting go of the coin. Thud. It lands perfectly in my shoe, and I once again slide it underneath my foot. Tonight's going to be a profitable night, to say the least. A flash of last night's incident passes through my mind, the clinking of silver dollars raining from my shoes to the ground as I watch helplessly from the loop-de-loop, and it brings a flush to my cheeks. But only for a moment. Then it is gone as soon as it comes.

\* \* \*

"I hear you like to dance." Shit. That slow, gravelly voice from behind me that has caused many-a-crooks to shudder makes a muscle jump in my jaw, and I square my shoulders before turning around to face Cosmo, the harsh light casting an ugly shadow on his hardened face. He brings up a Parodi to his lips, with his forefinger and thumb upturned, taking a big huff before blowing a billow of foul smelling smoke in my face.

I try my best not to make a sound, but my breath catches in my throat.

"Where'd you hear that?" I manage in an indifferent voice. What was a hundred bucks gonna do to this guy? I was an honest dealer, I don't know what else he wanted. A fella's gotta make a living someway.

"That's what they tell me. I'd like to see you dance."

"What?" I meet his dark, beady eyes in disbelief.

"I'd like to see you dance in dem shoes you got there."

"Look, Cosmo, I don't see what a couple dollars—" In a split second I find myself pinned against the wall, collar digging into my throat as Cosmo somehow lifts me off the ground

## Chapter Four

despite my being six inches taller than him.

"Those are *my* couple dollars." He growls, puffing on his cigarette with his free hand.

"I—I know. That's what—what I meant." I gasp out, spots dancing across my vision.

"I know that's what you meant. Now be a good boy, and don't do it again. Do you understand me?"

"Yeah—yeah, I understand." He lets me go, and my legs buckle beneath me as I catch my breath, gasping and sputtering. I hear his footsteps as he walks away, and I curse myself under my breath before standing and straightening my suit.

\* \* \*

Name: Dino Crocetti

Year: 1938

Age: 20

"Aren'tyoualooker?" The words tumble out of Costanzo's mouth without pause, and the blond dame whose scrawny arm he's grabbed yanks herself away from him, nose crinkling at his acrid breath. Costanzo stumbles, grabbing at a nearby lamppost for support. The girl looks a little wobbly herself, and wipes the back of her hand across her mouth disorientedly, smearing her scarlet lipstick.

I take the opportunity to put my arm under hers for support, and she glances up at me gratefully, pupils dilated. I've been

## The Crooner and The Comic

drinking too, but not nearly as much as Costanzo—yet—and this broad could be a lot of fun.

The whiskey feels like it's burning a hole in my throat as I take a big, exaggerated swig, dropping the bottle below the table as the server brings our food over. I burst into peals of what sounds like distant laughter when he leaves, and so does everyone else at the table, though I'm not sure why. I just feel like laughing.

"S—s—smells gooooood!" I exclaim, bringing my nose a mite too close to the plate. Costanzo groans, dropping his head on his arms.

"I think I'm gonna be sick . . ."

"Let's get outta here, Dino—maybe the clip joint!" Luca says excitedly.

"No, not the clip joint . . . let's go to the s—spables."

\* \* \*

My head is cleared almost as soon as Rocky breaks into a gallop, and I lean forward in the stirrups, an odd feeling of almost floating washing over me. I can't really see what's in front of me as the dusty wind whips past my face with a sharp sting. However, in my imagination I can see exactly where I am.

Dark shrubbery atop rocks that seem at some points a bright red, and at others a violet sort of color; a bright sky that seems to go on forever and ever. My hand moves from clutching Rocky's mane to my hat, tracing the almost impossibly long kettle curl brim with a dimpled grin. The distinct hoot from behind me sends a thrill through my body that ends with my hand reaching for my revolver. Without hesitation I send a

## Chapter Four

shot in that direction, arm taut to diminish the jerk of the gun as it fires.

Easing Rocky to a stop, I turn back triumphantly, hoping to catch sight of dark arms and legs splayed out against the rocks, further darkened by the scarlet blossoming across a still chest. My smile fades. No Indian, only a tree with one of its branches unfortunately broken off by the shot of a boy who thought he was Tom Mix. A chuckle escapes my lips.

# Chapter Five

Name: Joseph Levitch

Year: 1938

Age: 11

"It's ridiculous, really, what he's doing. I'm the main act, and people are actually leaving my show to see the silly antics of a little kid? What the hell's going on with this world?" Dad's words cut through the air like a knife, and I gasp instinctively, heart dropping.

"They'll get over it, but Danny, you've got to give the kid some credit, it's funny stuff." I don't know who he's talking to, but it's probably one of the other waiters he's doing his act with. The voices suddenly stop, and I pray they don't round the corner and see me. What a sight it would be—the

## Chapter Five

eavesdropping boy pressed against the wall with silent tears welling in his eyes.

"Whatever, I've got to get ready." Come dad's grumblings, and then two sets of footsteps growing softer. Once they're completely gone, I exhale in relief, sliding down the wall into a sitting position. He's angry with me doing the show? I don't understand. I thought I was doing a good job! Everyone else liked it . . . how come he never likes what I do?

A tightening in my chest makes me surge to my feet, go into my room and onto the balcony. The air is cool on my cheeks where my tears fell, and it smells damp outside. I start when a hand is placed on my shoulder, and I hear Charles' soft voice before I see him. "Hey, pal, what's on your mind?" He politely ignores my red-rimmed eyes and stares ahead, arm around my shoulder.

"Did you like my show?" I squeak out over the lump in my throat.

"Of course I did, Jer! You were very funny."

"You think so?"

"I know so. Matter of fact, if you were older, I would hire you to work here just like I've done for your dad." Somehow it makes the weird feeling in my chest go away, and I wipe my cheeks before smiling up at him. He smiles back and ruffles my hair before leaving. The feeling of his hand on my shoulder doesn't leave for a long while, and I close my eyes, pretending dad is standing behind me where Charles was.

* * *

"Lonnie! Hi!" Lonnie glances up from the book she's reading, dark eyes wide behind glasses.

"Oh, Jerry! Hi!" I can sense something flicker behind those beautiful eyes before she hurriedly stands, straightening her skirt. "I'm starving, do you want to go down to see what food they have for lunch?" She glances up at me hopefully for a moment before clearing her throat and clutching her book tightly to her chest.

"Sure." I say casually, but my heart is practically leaping out of my chest. She wants to eat lunch with *me*?

\* \* \*

Sunlight streams in from the great window at the end of the hall, littering the bright red carpet with stripes. As I move slowly through the hall, my bare feet are illuminated as they catch each stripe, wavering only slightly to keep balance. As I move closer towards the end of the hall, a muffled sound grows more and more distinct: someone's playing a record, but no one's singing yet, so I'm not sure which song. It has a great beat, though, and a kind of soft, underplayed melody, and I bounce a little on the balls of my feet as I leap from stripe to stripe.

Finally I get to the room I'm sure it's coming from, and when I glance up at the door I recognize it instantly as Lonnie's bedroom. I stand there for a moment, unsure, until the voice on the record begins, and I realize the song is "You're a Sweetheart." But that doesn't sound quite like Edythe Wright—it sounds like there are two people singing . . . wait, that's Lonnie singing! With an excited grin I knock on the door, just loud enough for her to hear.

The music abruptly stops, and the door opens a little from the inside so I can see part of her flushed face.

## Chapter Five

"Oh, hi, Jerry." She says, obviously embarrassed.
"Can I come in?"
"Well—"
"It's just that I heard you singing, and I think I can help you out a little." I offer, shoving my hands in my pockets.
"Alright, then, come in." She holds open the door, and I step into her room. It's quite nice, really, with a light pink bedspread neatly tucked in, and yellow, diamond-patterned wallpaper. The phonograph is sitting on her dresser, and seems to be the only thing not tidied up in the room, with chips in the wood and a discolored amplifier.
"Turn it back on and show me. You sounded pretty good." I encourage her, and she puts the record back on. I wasn't exactly lying, because she has a very pretty voice, but the instruments drown it out and make her strain too much to be heard. "I think I have an idea," I say once it's done, and Lonnie just raises her eyebrows and pushes her hair behind her ear, panting. "Why try to sing louder and better when you can just be her?"
"What do you mean?"
"Let me show you!" I say excitedly, and go over to the phonograph, moving the needle a little bit past the beginning of the record to start around when Edythe starts singing.
Lonnie watches me curiously as I bounce a little, trying to get in the mood of the song, and I turn to a teddy bear she has sitting on her pillow. Facing Lonnie makes me feel too . . . I don't know, scared, I guess. "You're a sweeeetheart, if there ever waaas one." Come the first lyrics, and I mouth them with my lips overtly puckered and eyebrows raised in mock imitation of some of the more fancy singers I've seen. Lonnie bursts out laughing gleefully, but I barely hear her—it's like I'm

there, performing for her, but at the same time a wondrous, consuming thrill runs through me.

\* \* \*

Name: Joseph Levitch

Year: 1938

Age: 12

The bell tinkling as we enter Gottlieb's drugstore is music to my ears—and warmth to my poor, frozen body. It feels like Lonnie and I have been walking for . . . well, for a really long time, and it's been snowing for at least as long.

We hop onto the stools at the counter and anxiously await our turn as Mr. Gottlieb serves sodas to the constant mass of people swarming in and out. Finally he takes our order, and though I've seen it a hundred times, I watch with avid fascination as he pumps the syrup into our glasses—my mouth's watering already—takes two big scoops of ice cream into each one, and tops them both off with a swirl of whipped cream and a glistening red cherry.

"OK, kids, this oughtta hold you." He hands them to us with a wink. "Don't tell nobody, but we've got the best sodas anywhere in New Jersey." I watch Lonnie's face light up as she eagerly takes a big scoop.

"Sure looks that way," I say, and then something occurs to me. With a proud smile I remark to Lonnie, "Did you know I

## Chapter Five

was a soda jerk once?" Lonnie glances up from her glass, lips tinged dark from the syrup.

"No—where?"

"At the Roxy drugstore in Irvington. I guess I wasn't too hot. I used to flip the ice cream up in the air and try to catch it in the cone. Sometimes I missed—hah!"

"Oh, no!" She seems both amused and dismayed, obviously not sure which one I want her to be.

"Yeah . . . I didn't like the job anyway." It's not true, but the more I say it, the more I'll believe it. I resist the urge to shudder as I remember the embarrassment of dropping the ice cream. Of being fired.

"Well—" Lonnie isn't sure how to respond, and just goes back to sipping her soda. I follow suit, no longer feeling so zany. I could keep a job if I really wanted to . . . Lonnie stops drinking for a moment and glances sideways at me, a strange expression on her pink-streaked face. "You're a funny one." I can tell from her tone she's not exactly complimenting me.

"Whatta ya mean?"

"The way your moods change. I think *you* know what I mean." She can see right through me. How is it that she notices what my own parents don't? An answer pops into my mind, but I'm not ready to hear it: they don't care enough to look.

I nod. Swallowing the lump that forms in my throat, I say nervously but carefully, "It's really nothin.' I get a little worried sometimes. Even here. I mean, it's great—but that's the trouble. When I'm having a good time, I always feel like some stupid thing will happen to make it bad."

"Like what?" One part of me is glad she's asking, glad she cares. But another part wants to hide.

"Well, like I remember things that happened, that's all."

### *The Crooner and The Comic*

"No, it's not all. Otherwise you wouldn't have mentioned it."

"Ah." I fall silent, shrugging it away. I hate the images that flash through my mind, twisting my stomach so I no longer want to drink my soda. Images of a lonely boy in a lonely house, cheeks wet with self-pitying tears. I never learn. I see myself standing on the front porch, rooted to the ground with fear well-masked as mom and dad pack their bags. They're leaving. They're leaving me again. I remember glancing to Brian beside me, who had walked home from school with me, and wondering if he understood. If he knew how I felt. If he had any idea my heart was being chipped away at, piece by piece.

"Are you all right?" Lonnie's voice pulls me from my thoughts. What's all right anymore?

"Yes." I lie with a broad grin. Why do I always do that?

When Lonnie's done with her drink (I lost my appetite), we go back into the frigid air, and I'm sure she won't keep on the topic when she says softly, "What's wrong, Joey?"

"Well, if you really want to know—" In an instant I'm overwhelmed with emotion, and I just have to get it out, so I scoop up a ball of snow in my hand. "It's just this. I'm by myself a lot." Ignoring the stinging, I throw it away so hard it's a wonder I don't dislocate my shoulder. "That's how it is. Because my parents aren't home much. They keep moving me from one place to another. A week here, a month there—sometimes with my Aunt Betty, or my Aunt Jean, my grandma in Brooklyn—I get tired of it. I get lonely." The words come out sort of choked, and I can't meet Lonnie's sympathetic eyes.

"Jerry. Listen to me. I'm sure your parents don't mean to—"

"Sure, sure." I cut her off bitterly, filled with anger. Like she

## Chapter Five

knows what my parents mean.

"They tell me the same thing. They don't mean to do it. They have to . . . There's no other way. But even if it's true, every time we're together they ignore me. I think—it's like this. You see your parents; you talk to them and you feel they understand you, but they don't. So all you see is a wall. A *big* wall. And that's what I've been thinking about."

I glance to her anxiously as we trudge side-by-side through the snow, but she just stares forward unseeingly. Oh no. Did I tell her too much? Will she not want to hang out with me anymore? Unable to cope with the silence, I say hurriedly, "You know what I once did?" She remains silent. Over the pounding of blood in my ears, I say, "OK. I'll tell you. When I was a little kid—about five years old—when they were away somewhere, I got so mad I threw my cat down the stairs. Killed it. You can get bad dreams from that, you know."

Lonnie stops in her tracks for a few moments, and I bite my lip. Why'd you say that? Then she calls out, "Wait up!" And when she catches up, she pants breathlessly, "Oh, Jerry—I wish I could help."

I wish you could, too.

## Chapter Six

Name: Dean Martin

Year: 1936

Age: 19

As I head slowly up the porch to the front door, feet aching something awful, an indistinguishable din of voices and laughs makes my heart sink. Damn it. After a whole long day of dealing, of course everyone has to be here for dinner.

   After taking a deep breath and squaring my shoulders, I open the door to everyone bustling throughout the living room, every adult with a wine glass in hand, and then some. I cross the room with my head slightly down, taking long, but relaxed strides. I hope no one notices me. I just want to go to bed.

   "Dino!" Damn it.

## Chapter Six

"Hey, Dino! Where've ya been?!" I turn around, a smile plastered on my face, to the warm embraces of aunts and uncles.

"Workin'." I say shortly, abruptly aware of the fact that my working at the Rex won't be too well received.

"Oh, really? Where?"

"The Rex." Muttered epithets in Italian and English alike, and disapproving glances follow, and I want to go upstairs. Not that I care too much what they think, I'm just tired, and don't want to deal with family. Mom's talking behind me with some of her sisters, who say, "Your son's gonna be a gangster. He's gonna die in the electric chair." I remember talking to mom and dad just the other day, explaining to them I don't gamble, and just work. I tried to explain it using *The Man Who Broke the Bank at Monte Carlo*—"Remember the guy with the stick? He wore the nice suit, the tie. He didn't gamble, he just worked. Well, that's me."

Finally I hear mom's response: "You're crazy. My son's gonna be a star." I smile to myself. I knew mom believed in me. She always has. She's the only one.

\* \* \*

### The Crooner and The Comic

Name: Dino Crocetti

Year: 1940

Age: 23

*Dino, why are you a singer? Why don't you just work at the steel mills? That's a dependable job, you can support a family that way.* The questions harass me. They won't leave me alone. It seems I hear it from everyone I know.

My answer is always the same: "I dunno, I just like to sing." But that one sunny afternoon coming home from school always leaps to the front of my mind. I don't know how old I was, probably ten or eleven, and I was leaping up the front steps to the house when footsteps echoed throughout the air. I turned around, curious, and saw dozens of men trudging through the streets, coming back from the steel mills.

I remember watching as they came closer, expressionless faces dark with soot and grease, lunch pails swinging from tired, tired arms. Their only dignity was the suit jacket each worker wore—despite how dirty and ragged it had become. Nowadays it seemed like even the homeless were dressed nicely. But the worst part as they marched past me wasn't the dirt, wasn't the clothing, wasn't even their slow, labored steps and hunched over backs. It was their eyes.

Seemingly without exception they would gaze at me for a second with heavy-lidded, unseeing eyes haunted by something unspeakable, tired beyond their years—eyes in which

## Chapter Six

the spark of life, the spark of dreams, has been extinguished.

*I'm never going to work there,* I vowed to myself that day. *I won't let them take away my life. That's not living. That's surviving—barely.*

# Chapter Seven

Name: Joseph Levitch

Year: 1939

Age: 13

This is it. This is the day I've been waiting for. It's March 16, my birthday. But not just any birthday, my 13th birthday. The only day of my life where I get to be the one everyone looks at, everyone smiles at and claps for, and everyone loves.

My eyes fly open to the comforting, tantalizing aroma of Bisquick and syrup, poached eggs, and the sharp, but sweet tang of sliced oranges. Excitement brings me to my senses immediately, and I throw off the covers, leaping onto my feet. The floor is freezing, but I'm so eager I don't care enough to put on my slippers.

## Chapter Seven

Bounding into the kitchen, I see Grandma Sarah placing two plates at the table sitting just a few feet from the oven and fridge. I sit down, fingers unconsciously tracing the chipped metal edge of the table. Grandma looks down at me, pleasantly surprised, and exclaims, "Joey! I was just going to wake you up! Happy birthday, my love!" She wraps me in a big hug, kissing me on the cheek, and a feeling of complete comfort and safety washes over me. She loves me.

'Thanks, Grandma. I'm so excited for the Bar Mitzvah!"

"Of course you are. It's going to be a very special time, so keep the memories of it safe here." She gestures towards my forehead, and I nod, practically beaming. My stomach rumbles, and she laughs cheerily, putting a fork in my hand.

"Eat, Joey! It's your day to enjoy yourself. You're a man now!"

That's right. It's my day. The best day.

\* \* \*

This is the worst day. I want to die. I want to shrink into the size of an ant and be crushed and never have to face anyone again. But I'm not that lucky as I stand in the middle of the nearly empty shul, reciting my portion of the Haftarah with a voice that at any moment threatens to break. But I can't let it.

As I feel the heat begin to rise to my cheeks, and my eyes sting, I clench my fist at my side, nails cutting crescents into my palm, until my eyes and throat are clear. I can't meet eyes with the only person gazing up at me with adoration; the only person here at all—Grandma. It's too shameful, too embarrassing to admit that I'm a nothing. I'm jerky, and I'm nothing.

Once it's all over I sit in the car numbly, staring out the

### The Crooner and The Comic

window as Grandma drives me back to her house where the reception was supposed to be.

"They'll come. Don't worry, Joey. They'll come. They must have a perfectly good reason for being late." But they never do, I want to say to her. Shout to her. Scream to her. But I just sit there silently facing the window, misting it with ragged breath, and smudging it with tears shed.

As we cross the long concrete walk up to the front door, I swipe at my eyes with the back of my hand; wanting there to be people to greet me, but not exactly expecting anyone given the last reception I received.

However, when Grandma swings the door open, I am shocked by the smattering of applause and shouted congratulations that greet me. My feet are rooted to the ground, and my eyes eagerly roam the crowd for those two faces; those two wonderful, sweet, adoring faces . . . that are not there. All excitement fades away almost immediately, and I shuffle in with red-rimmed eyes.

I somehow manage to endure all of the pleasantries and congratulations, and end up sitting in a thatch-backed chair in the corner of the room—but the worst part of it all comes when they do arrive. Mom and dad waltz through the doorway in all their splendor, all smiles and laughter. No 'I'm sorry's for being late, no rush to find me and sweep me up in a congratulatory hug; a happy and proud hug. Instead they bask in the glory of neighbors and relatives telling them how proud they must be their son is now a man, that he finally got his bar mitzvah, that they did a great job organizing this reception. But they don't deserve any of it.

\* \* \*

## Chapter Seven

That evening when everybody has been gone for hours, grandma is sitting at the sewing table working on a new pair of pants for me.

I know where she is, but she doesn't know where I am—she hasn't even gone looking for me yet. I bring my knees to my chest and place my chin on my knees so the light from the kitchen doesn't touch me. With the wall on one side of me, and the back of the couch on the other, I feel safe. Lonely, but safe.

Why didn't mom and dad come to the ceremony when they said they would? They always forget to see me. Forget. What a funny word. It seems as if everyone forgets about me. The dumb, jerky kid.

I'm alone. Used to it by now, but it still hurts. It hurts bad. No matter how many times mom lets me down, no matter how many times she's not there when I want her; when I need her, I can't help missing her like she's a part of me. The part of me that tells me I'm loved. The part of me that holds me tight and strokes my hair. The part of me that tells me everything's going to be alright.

I can't help the warm tears that escape my eyes in a torrent, but I clap my hand over my mouth, stifled sobs racking my body. Nevertheless grandma hears me, and peeks over the top of the couch, lips curled into a sympathetic smile.

"Oh, Joey, come here. I'm right here, you're going to be okay." Sniffling, I wipe my eyes and crawl over the couch into her arms. Hiding my face in her neck, I feel a strong but gentle hand rubbing my back up, down, up, down. My breathing slowly returns to normal, and I untwist my fingers from her sweater, sitting up.

"Can I stay up while you sew?" The small, frightened plea

## The Crooner and The Comic

from a child.

"Of course you can." The confident, reassuring answer from an adult, followed by an amused smile.

I crawl underneath the table, head on my hands as I wearily watch grandma's feet press the pedals. As my eyes grow heavy, I let them close, still listening to the sound of the pedals and the needle whirring. They're nice sounds, comforting sounds. They keep on going in that rhythm, and I know that for a little while everything's going to be okay . . .

\* \* \*

Name: Joey Levitch

Year: 1940

Age: 14

That red light above the emergency entrance of the hospital glitters ominously; threateningly. It has all the power in the world. Please be okay, Grandma. Please. I can't live without you. You're the only one in the world who cares for me. But even *you* pity me.

I tear myself away from the window, away from the glaring light. A thousand wonderful, warm memories flood through my mind of Grandma and me. Cooking in the kitchen. Talking at the table. When she gave me that wonderfully thoughtful baseball cap for my birthday—I thought I'd never take it off.

Shaking my head to come back to the present, I look back up

## Chapter Seven

to the window. The hospital entrance is dark. The light's gone. With trembling hands I grab the phone book and desperately leaf through the thin pages until I find the hospital's number.

"Can you tell me how Sarah Rothberg is, please?"

"She has expired." An emotionless female voice says. My heart drops, but I ask with the most hopeful of voices, "Does that mean she's getting better?"

"No . . ." There's a pause on the other end, and then the voice says awkwardly, "I'm sorry. She died."

My throat goes tight, and my mouth runs dry . . . She died? Grandma? My Grandma Sarah? No, it can't be. She's the only one who loves me. Who asks me about school. Who asks me how I feel . . . and now she's gone, and I'm all alone.

# Chapter Eight

~~~~~~

Name: Dean Martin

Year: 1941

Age: 24

Such a smile would have buckled the knees of many a fella, but not me. I finish out the song strong, with only a few stolen glances giving away my interest.
   Stepping back from the microphone, I lean towards Eddie, who is cleaning his trombone before the next song, and ask with a low voice, "Who's that dame over there?" Eddie glances up, searching the crowd, although I don't know how he can see with all that sweat dripping from his dark forehead and into his eyes.
   "What dame? Dino, it's a full house!"

## Chapter Eight

"The pretty one in the back row, with the white dress." I glance again in her direction, and she's talking to some people who seem to be her folks. Eddie cranes his neck until he turns back to me, a glimmer of recognition in his eyes.

"Oh! Don't you know who that is? That's Mayor Lausche and his daughter. Come on, I'll introduce you."

"You know, I'm not so sure . . . " I take out my pocket square and dab at the moisture gathering above my lips, returning to the microphone. She'll probably be gone tomorrow, so I'll just have to be satisfied from afar.

**Two Days Later**

"Do you want someone to show you around town? You've been here for a couple days now, haven't ya?"

"What, do you use that line on all the starry-eyed tourists here at the hotel?" She turns around to face me, red lips curling up into a smile dripping with sarcasm.

"Only the pretty ones."

"Well, thanks, but no thanks." She moves to walk away, but I stop her with my hand lightly on her arm.

"At least tell me your name, darling." I croon, undeterred by her coldness.

"I'm Betty. See you around, Dean." With that, she turns on her hot pink heels and leaves just as I open my mouth to tell her my name.

I watch her leave with a crooked grin, shaking my head. I know that she likes me; soon she'll admit it.

\* \* \*

## *The Crooner and The Comic*

Name: Dean Martin

Year: 1941

Age: 24

Heat rises to my cheeks, and my palms are clammy as I wipe them on my slacks. Why the hell am I so nervous? It's just the moment that I'm going to see if Betty's the one. The one? That's such bull, but that's what everyone tells me anyway.

The soft tugging on my sleeve pulls me from my thoughts, and I glance down to Betty, who slips her hand in mine.

"So, I guess it's time to meet some of your real friends—I hope they have some embarrassing stories about little Dino." Betty teases as we walk into the cigar shop, smile bringing a rosy flush to her prominent cheeks.

"I don't think you'll be so lucky. Now watch this. I'm sure you've never seen one of these in Chester, now have ya?" I say softly as I nod to Stogie, who's sitting behind the counter with a hardened expression, and watch Betty's awed expression in amusement when we go through a hidden cubby into the back room.

"You used to work here?"

"Yep." I study her closely, not sure if she's going to turn up her nose or break into a smile. Her eyes dart back and forth from person to person, analyzing the whole room like a seasoned Dick Tracy, until she lets out a soft sigh and turns to me expressionlessly.

"I like it. It's . . . a little rough around the edges, but if I were a man, I'd probably spend time here."

## Chapter Eight

"I'm glad you're not a man."

"Hm. Are you, now?"

"Mhm." I murmur, leaning down to press my lips gently against hers. That is, until the whole damn place fills with shouts alerting the entire town to my return.

"Dino!"

"Hey, Dino's back!"

Before I know it, we're surrounded, and Betty's hand tightens around mine. Lighting a cigarette, I let it hang lazily between my lips before introducing her to everyone. My face doesn't betray the quickening of my heart in the moment of silence between their meeting her and their reaction.

"You picked well, Dino. She'll certainly be one to keep you in check."

"Shut up." I playfully hit Eddie in the arm, and he laughs, shaking his head.

"No, but I'm only joking, Dino. Betty's great." It feels like a weight is lifted from my chest, and I grin, squeezing Betty's hand reassuringly. It looks like I was right after all.

# Chapter Nine

Name: Joseph Levitch

Year: 1942

Age: 16

Snap. With one final moan, the saw breaks cleanly in half around the nail poking through the wood that I was a little too slow to see. Shit. I try to cover my growing dread with a snicker, and as my classmates begin to glance over at the scene, nervous laughter fills the classroom until Mrs. Reese turns around. Everyone knows what's happening as she pushes up her horn-rimmed glasses and closes her eyes, shoulders rising and falling once in an inaudible sigh.
"Go to Mr. Herder's office, Joseph. Now." Before getting out of my seat, I face the rest of my classmates and cross my

## Chapter Nine

eyes, lower lip jutting out in mock concern. If I didn't make fun, I'd probably cry. They erupt into peals of laughter, and I slink off to Mr. Herder's office. The principal.

As I sit on the wooden bench outside of his office, feet tapping the ground restlessly, I bite my lip. This is the fifth time this month, and I don't exactly cherish those meetings with a big, red-faced German man who needs a life of his own.

The door creaks open, and out steps Mr. Herder, glancing on both sides of him like a policeman patrolling the street before motioning me in. He has me sit in a chair that's far too small for me, and my legs jut out awkwardly as I stare up at Mr. Herdner across the desk. His small, watery eyes squint disapprovingly, and he says gruffly, "What are you, a wise guy?"

What is he, a moron? He really thinks I broke the saw on purpose? Wouldn't I do something a little more extravagant if I wanted to break something? I sit there silently, almost surprised at the rage that blossoms inside of me, sending a wave of heat to my face. "Why is it only the Jews—" Mr. Herder is cut off mid sentence by my fist connecting with his mouth—the sickening crack as I bust in a few of his teeth follows instantly.

For a split second I regret plotzing. But then I remember. He's a meshugener. He asked for it.

\*\*\*

*The Crooner and The Comic*

Name: Jerry Lewis

Year: 1944

Age: 18

"Hey, girlie, you should have dinner with me tonight." I lean against the side of the stage, eyes meeting hers unblinkingly.

"Are you for real?" She hisses, a smile plastered on her face towards the audience until she marches fully off the stage after her number, breezing past me. I watch her stalk away, feathers from her costume that jut from her hips swaying from side to side. I grin, shrugging off the embarrassment that threatens to wash over me as usual. She'll come around.

About a minute later it's my turn to perform, but throughout the whole song I'm mimicking, I cast sideways glances in her direction. To my pleasure, I find her watching my act with keen interest, all while whispering to one of her dancer friends and playing with her gorgeous black curls.

Finally I'm done, and the audience claps politely while I slink off the stage in my Idiot way.

"Alright, then." The girl says just loud enough for me to hear as I pass, and I turn around, straightening my zoot suit with an exaggerated grin.

"What was that?" I ask in my Idiot voice—a defense, perhaps—but irregardless of the reason, I use it.

"I . . . said alright. You can take me out." Her voice is rich and soft, and her shining red lips are full as she purses them

## Chapter Nine

hesitantly.

"What changed your mind?" I ask normally, heart jumping as she smiles shyly.

"Well, you're not like all the other guys. You're just a scared, silly kid. Like me."

It feels like a punch in the gut until I look into her chestnut eyes, and I kow she meant it as a compliment.

"Well, let's go to Papa Joe's. They have great ice cream. Us kids can share some tootie fruitie." Shaking her head, she asks me with that polite voice of hers when I'm planning on taking her.

"6 tomorrow night." With that, although I'd like to stay and talk to her, or just look at her, I skip away. Just being the kid she thinks I am.

### 6 PM the next day

Oh shit. I'm late. I give the girl—whatever her name is—one last, slow kiss before murmuring, "Sorry, but I've got to go." I stand up from the couch and put on my coat.

"Are you sure?" She asks, a mischievous rather than disappointed expression on her face as she stands as well, stepping close to me to straighten my tie.

"As much as I'd like to stay, I've got a date I should have been at 30 minutes ago."

"Of course you do. See you later?"

"Sure."

As I round the corner where Papa Joe's is, I shoot a glance through the window, and to my relief, Patti is sitting in one of the booths near the back, looking very beautiful but very bored, shuffling a few grains of salt around on the brilliant red table with a toothpick.

"Hey, I'm so sorry I'm late." I say breathlessly once I've jogged across the room over to her booth.

"It's okay. What kept you?" She says sweetly with what seems to be a forced smile on her face. My heart drops as I sit down across from her, and I stammer, "Well, I—I was, uh . . . "

"I think I've got my answer." Patti reaches across the table to tug my collar from beneath my suit coat, her slender fingers just brushing across my jaw as she withdraws her hand. Glancing down, I realize there are lipstick stains on it. Before I can react, she's snapping her purse shut and slipping her gloves back on.

"Wait!" The word flies from my mouth before I even think it, and my hand loosely grips her wrist, pleading. "Don't go. Please. I wasn't thinking, and I'm sorry. Just . . . stay." Patti withdraws her hand from mine, staring at me with those hardened eyes of hers, and I honestly have no idea what she's thinking.

"I don't know why, but I guess I'll stay. I already ordered dinner, anyhow." I sigh in relief and smile abashedly at her, tugging my suit back over my collar with one quick motion.

"Tell me about yourself. I mean, how did you become a singer? Oh, and how old are you, anyway?" I ask, the thought popping into my mind that she might be under 18, but at the same time I doubt it because there's something about her that seems so much older than that.

"I'm 24." She hides her smile with her kerchief at my reaction, and then proceeds to tell me her story. At first I don't really listen, and just look at her for a long while. The black curls that cascade to her shoulders in almost unruly locks that I want to run my hands through. The big doe eyes framed by

## Chapter Nine

long lashes—are those fake? The perfectly red, dovetailed lips whose lipstick must have been applied just as I came in.

Then I stop looking to listen for a moment, and boy is that a mistake. I hear how her mom used to beat her and such, and I feel a pang in my chest—is it sympathy? Well, sure, I'm no monster. But there's something else. Jealousy? No . . . Disappointment, perhaps. It makes sense, I know how eager I always am to tell my story to some new broad, who'll look at me with sad eyes and pet my hair like they can make up for the person who should have done that but didn't. I guess in a way the story explains the behavior, so the other girls don't mind that I go out with someone else—*he doesn't know what he's doing; he's just a scared little boy*. But there's no doing that with Patti. It's almost like she's doing this because she can see right through me. She found me out.

Heat rising to my cheeks, I take one last sip of my coffee before making a show of glancing up at the clock and sighing, "Gee, look at the time. I've really got to get going. There's rehearsals tomorrow morning."

"Oh, well that's too bad. I had a good time tonight, Jerry."

"Yeah, me too, Patti." I manage a small smile, and I swear she looks amused for a moment as I stand up and begin to move towards the door.

"I'll see you later."

"Yeah."

**2 Months Later**

"Alright, stop here, that'll be fine." I call out to the driver, leaning forward in my seat as the taxi rolls up to the front of the Holland Hotel.

## The Crooner and The Comic

"Oh, I wish you didn't have a show to get to." Patti murmurs, a mock frown on her face. I lightly trace her cheeks with my forefinger and push the corner of her lips up into a smile.

"I won't be gone for that long. I'll see you tonight, Esther. I love you." *Esther.* I love calling Patti by her real name. It's mine.

"I love you too. You'll be great out there, darling." She looks at me warmly for a moment before kissing me on the cheek, glancing furtively at the driver looking at us through the rearview mirror. I nod and step out of the taxi, coming face to face with Irving.

"You better hurry or you'll be late for the first show." Irving says hurriedly, crossing his arms with a disapproving glance at his watch. Unable to be shaken from the warm feeling almost like floating coming over me, I grin broadly and hold out my left hand.

"Is that any way to greet a friend? Where's the congratulations?" Irving takes one look at the ring and turns his head away, chewing the inside of his cheek.

"Well, say something!" I would've thought Irving out of all people would have been excited. Irving lets out a long breath before muttering, "Your parents are upstairs."

"Oh, shit."

* * *

"You didn't! You didn't! How dare you?! You're making me sick!" Mom shouts, sinking into the nearest chair with fingers splayed at her collarbone. Swallowing, I protest, "Come on, mom! She's a good person!"

Completely ignoring me, mom continues with her tirade,

## Chapter Nine

"What did I raise you for? To run off with a Catholic?!" Shaking her head, eyes burning, she says darkly, "If your grandmother was alive, she'd drop dead." My body goes cold, and I gaze at her disbelievingly through blurred vision.

"That's not fair." I manage over the lump that forms in my throat.

"What you did wasn't fair."

"Come on, just wait until you meet—"

"Just go! Go! Get the hell out of here!" Dad interrupts me, shooting to his feet with a vein pulsing from his temple. Hands balled into fists, I stand there staring at them for a moment before shaking my head and running downstairs to the backstage. I knew this was going to happen, so why does it still hurt so much?

**6 Months Later**

This isn't how it was supposed to be. Marriage, that is. I'm the man of the household, and I'm the one who's supposed to be supporting Patti. But now she's the one who's with the Tommy Dorsey Band. She's the one sending me the checks. I'm a nobody. Why would she love a nobody? Why would she stay with someone like me when she can be with someone wealthy or famous?

I'm just a schliemel bumming around.

I stop walking and sit on a bench a few feet away. The feeling is so overwhelming, so excruciating that I want to scream into the night air. But I just scrub a hand over my face and gaze out at the park tinted orange by street lights through blurry vision.

For New York, I'm surprised it's so desolate, with only the

occasional car creeping by. Otherwise it's like I'm alone in a forest, dry leaves rattling with each gust of wind, and some of the larger trees groaning beneath the weight of their fully clothed branches.

    I wish I could stay here. It's peaceful, and I don't have to face anyone else. I don't have to disappoint them like I always do.

# Chapter Ten

Name: Dean Martin

Year: 1944

Age: 27

"Waaaayy Maaaariee . . . way marie . . . Quanto sonno, agiu perso per te!" I croon, watching in amusement as all the dames in the room eye my fingers running lightly over the base of the microphone.
  "What are you, F-4 or somethin'?" Someone from a ringside table bellows, and although I can't exactly make out his whole face, I can see the drunken red haze in his eyes before I glance away in disdain. Although most of the audience drops their gaze and falls into an uncomfortable silence, a few men who share the fat-head's sentiments laugh out-loud, protected by

## The Crooner and The Comic

the spotlight nearly blinding me.

"Chooch." I mutter under my breath, upper lip curling in scorn. I know he couldn't have understood what I said, but I catch sight of the hand that slips into his pocket in response. Without hesitation, I push the microphone out of the way and dive right on top of the son of a bitch. We crash onto the floor together, the pounding of blood in my ears drowning out the startled cries from the crowd. As soon as we hit the floor I knock the guy's wrist into the ground so the switchblade flies out of his hand and lands a few feet away.

I grip his pomaded hair and slam his face into the ground so I can hear the snap of his nose with a crack. He goes limp, but things aren't over yet as hands begin seizing my jacket and all I can smell is breath that could get me drunk all by itself. Struggling to my feet, I force myself through the crowd by swinging blindly and hoping I don't hit a dame.

Finally I'm hit by a gust of wind, and I know I'm out safe. Head spinning, I stumble into the street as the bouncer and a few of the other staff members stop them from coming out after me.

"Disgraziat'."

\* \* \*

## Chapter Ten

Name: Dean Martin

Year: 1944

Age: 27

The sight of the boisterous sign titled "Nedick's" makes my stomach growl pitifully, and I wish for once—just for once—I could have a full meal. But I know wishful thinking gets you nowhere but in a lot of trouble.

"Do you two want the usual?"

"Yep." Sonny replies to the waitress, and he sits down beside me at the counter, hungrily eyeing the breakfasts of the people around us.

"Are you sure you're ready for tonight?" I say slyly, a grin playing on my lips.

"What are you talkin' about? I'm the one who actually won more than one fight." Sonny shakes his head at me and lifts a fist with bumpy fingers and knuckles shining with scars that didn't quite heal right. "This baby gave a lot of people a nose like yours."

I shove his arm only half playfully, and the warm, rich scent of coffee turns my head. Set before me are a glass of orange juice, a doughnut, and a cup of coffee. With precise calculation I scarf down half the glass, half of the doughnut, and half of the coffee. Glancing around warily, I wipe the corner of my mouth with my pocket square before looking to Sonny, who says casually, "You'd better go sign those contracts."

"Finish this for me." I respond generously, but I feel much less generous than I sound. I'm downright starving. Giving the rest of the meal a final wistful glance, I stand up and stroll away.

### Later that Night

"Give it to him!"

"Yeah, really make him bleed!" Shouts come from all around us, enveloping us in a dingy cloud befitting a place with busted marquee lights and a persistent stench of blood and sweat.

"Don't you dare, Sonny. I'm older than you, remember that." I mutter to him as we circle each other in the ring, bouncing lightly to and fro on the balls of our feet. He rolls his eyes, bare fists raised in front of him in the instinctive stance of a seasoned fighter.

I give him a quick shot in the mouth before darting back away from his reach. After a few moments of failed swings on both sides, he manages to place a blow to my stomach, and oxygen evades my grasp.

Now angry, as soon as I catch my breath, I stride forward brazenly, eyes flashing, and drive Sonny back with punches square in the jaw until I realize just where Sonny is a second too late. The final blow sends Sonny reeling back into the window just behind him, which completely shatters. He manages to grab a hold of the metal blinds and dangles helplessly. It occurs to me we're six floors up.

With a frightening coldness washing over me, I race over to Sonny and grab his wrist, pulling him back into the room. Finally he's on the ground inside, and we both lie there, chest

## Chapter Ten

heaving—his back and chest covered in blood from the glass shards of the window. Guess I'm stronger than I think.

## Chapter Eleven

Names: Dean Martin and Jerry Lewis

Year: 1945

Ages: 28 and 18

Sotto voce? Why do they always put that kind of crap on billboards no one understands? Sotto voce? What was wrong with JERRY LEWIS: SATIRICAL IMPRESSIONS IN PANTOMIMICRY? Oh yeah, now Jerry remembers.
 His eyes wander up the board to the image of him in his all-too-expensive suit and a smile on his face that's trying a little too hard to be suave. Geez, when did he get that weird-looking? Jerry shrugs to himself. That's why he's a comedian, not an actor.
 Ding. The elevator doors slide open a few feet away from

## Chapter Eleven

him, and his gaze follows the stream of people into the lobby, trying to catch a glimpse of someone worth looking at. Nope. They're just a group of older ladies . . . and *him*. Something is so familiar and . . . breathtaking about the guy that stands a head above the ladies—what is he, 6'4" or something'?

He saunters through the lobby, a short cigarette pinched in large, manly hands. As the man comes closer to passing him, Jerry catches a closer glimpse of his features—long, rugged face, great profile: thick, dark brows and eyelashes. And a suntan in March! How'd he manage that?

As he strides past Jerry, his wavy, coal-black hair is somehow perfectly tousled by the breeze that passes through the hotel entrance just ahead. Jerry's glance falls to the man's shining red leather shoes that just scream successful. The fella pauses for a moment at the entrance to chew fat with the doorman before disappearing into the bustling crowd for good.

Jerry waits a second before walking up to the doorman casually and asking, "Who was that?"

"Dean Martin."

"He looks important."

"Could be. He sings on WMCA."

"No kidding. What program?"

The doorman shrugs and reverts his gaze to the approaching ladies from the elevator. Jerry takes the hint and walks back to his place by the lounge. His mind was racing with this Dean Martin who, in one moment, replaced the awe-inspiring legend that was Danny Lewis.

Dean had all but one passing thought of the funny-looking Jewish kid gawking at him like every other dame in the building.

## The Crooner and The Comic

\*\*\*

Names: Dean Martin and Jerry Lewis

Year: 1945

Ages: 28 and 18

Noise swirls around Jerry, drowning him—the distant laughter of children scurrying from their mothers, the rumble of engines, the wind whistling by him that tugs at his coat—but anything was better than surrendering himself to the thoughts trying to creep their way into his mind.

"Hey, Kid, that fella over there's Dean Martin. Here, I'll introduce you to him." Sonny exclaims suddenly, pointing at the man across the street at Broadway and Fifty-fourth coming their way.

"Oh, okay." Jerry says with a nonchalant shrug, pretending his heart isn't hammering in his chest. He watches Dean come closer to them, and stares at his Harry Horseshit coat and red and white pimp shoes.

"Hey, Dino!" Sonny says to Dean once he and a short, older man with cool eyes stop in front of him and Jerry. "How ya doin', Lou?" With a slight, disinterested nod, Lou acknowledges Jerry. Excitedly turning to Dean, Sonny says, "Dino, I want you to meet a very funny kid, Jerry Lewis."

Dean grins lazily—but warmly—at Jerry, extending a big, calloused hand. Jerry takes it and stares transfixed for a moment as his hand disappears under Dean's paw. Dropping

## Chapter Eleven

his hand, Jerry smiles to himself. He likes Dean immediately, and he can tell Dean's glad to meet him too—that's a first.

As they stand there, Jerry's mind works furiously to come up with something to say—anything to say. He feels this overwhelming need to make Dean smile at him again.

"You workin'?" Jerry asks eagerly. There it is, that million-dollar smile.

"Oh, this 'n' that, you know," Dean says, an instantly recognizable Southern lilt to his voice—gee, he could almost pass for Crosby and Jerry hasn't even heard him sing yet! "I'm on WMCA radio, sustaining. No bucks, just room." Jerry watches Dean closely, sees the sun-kissed skin, the faint trace of a healing surgical cut on the bridge of his nose, and the crinkling at the edges of his soft, brown eyes as he smiles.

Jerry's sure that *there's* a guy who's got it all together, someone who doesn't have a care in the world. Only the subtle narrowing of Dean's eyes gives away the ocean of debt he was barely wading through. "How 'bout you?" Dean asks Jerry, who nods enthusiastically and answers with a voice just a mite lower than usual, "I'm just now finishing my eighth week at the Glass Hat. In the Belmont Plaza."

"Really? I live there."

"At the Glass Hat?"

"No, at the Belmont. It's part of my radio deal." Dean says with the pride of one admitting to living in the Ritz-Carlton.

# Chapter Twelve

Names: Martin and Lewis

Year: 1946

Ages: 28 and 19

"You call this a room? Ow!" Jerry curses under his breath, hopping back and forth on his feet after banging his shin against the bedside table on his way back from the john. Dean chuckles, but it doesn't reach his eyes as he lies stretched out on the bed.
"What, that bad?" Sonny asks Dean with amusement.
"She had a roommate. Where the hell can a fella get lucky in peace and quiet in this damn town?" Rolling his eyes, Dean sits up and lets out a soft hiss of air between his teeth. Drawing a cigarette from his pocket, he leans forward as Sonny whips

## Chapter Twelve

out a lighter. Jerry's sure it's a normal cigarette, but between Dean's stiff fingers, it seems at least half its size.

Clenching the cigarette between his teeth, Dean gets off the bed and pours himself a Scotch. Swallowing it in one gulp, he sighs and relaxes his shoulders before turning to them with a cocked eyebrow. "You're not gonna let me drink this all by myself, are ya?"

Jerry shakes his head, offering a small smile, but he knows the strongest drink he's had is a hot cocoa. Still, he knows he can't pass up a Scotch from *Dean*. Holding up the bathroom tumbler to his lips, Jerry glances away, the strong smell of alcohol burning his nose and throat. But as Dean plays Sasquatch on his record player, Jerry tries to look as though he's taken a few gulps of the stuff.

### 4 hours later—1 AM

Sonny slouches over at the foot of the bed, mouth open in a silent snore. Jerry's on his stomach on the floor, enthralled as he gazes up at Dean lying on the bed, who's telling him about his reasons for leaving Steubenville. Only an occasional slur of words gives away the fact that the half-empty glass in his hand is his third—or was it his fourth?

As he listens, Jerry isn't tired enough to miss the 'I don't give a damn about anyone or anything' that practically gushes from Dean's words, but a small part of him wonders. Wonders if there's bitterness behind that easy smile. Wonders if there's a heart that got broken somewhere along the line.

"They call me the 'Boy with the Tall, Dark, and Handsome Voice.'" Dean says, gazing up at the ceiling that's stained with God knows what, and smiles grimly to himself. He knows there's not much to it. Just a bunch of doe-eyed broads who think he's all that because of the way he just is. He never did no training or nothin', he just likes to sing, and he happens to have a face that was nice to look at.

Jerry, on the other hand, agrees completely with the title. Who wouldn't? He wishes he could have just half of what Dean has. Not only could he get any dame he looked at, he was a man's man.

Dean breaks from his trance and pulls out a couple of pictures from the dress shirt he stripped off in favor of a grey beater.

"And look at me, a family man, too." He hands them down to Jerry, who marvels at the picture that looks like a promo for an MGM movie. A real family man, huh? He sure had the family, but the man doesn't exactly act like he has one. Then again, no one in this business does.

"Gee, she's real pretty, Dean."

"Yeah, she is. Look at my kids there, too! That's Craig, Claudia, and Gail." He points them out and glances to Jerry's face for his reaction before settling back on the bed.

"I've got a kid on the way, too." Jerry pipes up, an excited grin on his face as Dean bolts up with a shocked expression. It isn't something he anticipates seeing often, so Jerry studies Dean's face for a moment just to remember.

"You're kiddin' me. How old are you, pally?"

"I just turned nineteen," Jerry begins, a sudden blush crossing his cheeks. "But I've been married to Patti since October, and we have a baby due in July." Feeling suddenly like he's talking too much about himself, he abruptly asks, "How old are you?"

"Gettin' up there. About to turn twenty eight." Dean says slowly. When did he get that old? Oh well, he knew life would

## Chapter Twelve

be like this, so might as well enjoy it while it lasts.
    Jerry counts the numbers in his head. Twenty eight. Nine years older than him. Dean could be his big brother. He always wanted a big brother.

\* \* \*

Names: Dean Martin and Jerry Lewis

Year: 1946

Ages: 28 and 19

"Here, I'll give you five bucks if you just let me borrow your uniform." Jerry whispers anxiously to the waiter busily arranging food on a platter.
    "What? Why? I'm working, if you haven't noticed."
    "It's for my act! I promise I'll give it back in twenty minutes at the very most—besides, five bucks is way more than you should get for it!" The waiter, a tall but scrawny teen with flaming red hair and just as shockingly blue eyes, bites his lip in hesitation before relenting and holding his hand out.
    "Thanks, pally! You won't regret it!" Jerry breaks out into a relieved smile and slaps the five dollars into his upturned palm before helping him strip off his coat and bright red bowtie.
    A circle of white light illuminates a part of the stage against Dean's strong frame as he holds the microphone to his lips with just the faintest touch. The rest of the stage is in shadow, so Jerry easily sneaks in from the wings without anyone noticing

him.

His hands tremble slightly, and a nervous grin plays at his lips—why is he so nervous? He hasn't felt that way since he first started performing officially three years ago. Oh yeah, because he was about to interrupt *Dean Martin* in the midst of his song—a song that he would listen to for hours on end if he had the chance.

Alright. Now's the time—now or never. With a deep, ragged breath, Jerry forces himself to cough loudly, hacking and wheezing like his life depended on it. On cue, he's abruptly thrust into a light that makes the whole world go white for a moment. Also as if on cue, it's like a gear shifts in his mind, and all of the nervousness fades away into the background as he shouts at the top of his lungs in his Idiot voice, "Who ordered steak?!"

The music comes to a dysfunctional stop, and so does Dean. For a second as Dean stands there as straight as a board, Jerry's stomach twists. What if he had misjudged things? What if Dean got mad at him?

But instead of yelling insults or furiously shoving him off the stage, Dean turns his head slowly to the opposite side of the stage Jerry was standing on as if looking for him, and surveys the audience, who by this time are practically falling out of their seats laughing, to finally let his gaze rest on the frightened monkey who had ruined his song. Although Jerry expected to find anger in Dean's eyes, he finds playful amusement tugging at the corners of Dean's lips. He feels that everything is alright. In one moment, a man finds a boy who will teach him to open his heart, and a boy finds a man who will be the missing piece to his heart—the piece is frayed and worn around the edges, but it fits.

## Chapter Thirteen

Names: Dean Martin and Jerry Lewis

Year: 1946

Ages: 28 and 19

Cheers. Louder than either the Organ Grinder or the Monkey had ever heard in their lives. It's all Jerry can hear, all he can think about, and his heart races madly in his chest to keep up with the applause until he opens his eyes and the curtains coming down to the stage envelop them in darkness.

\* \* \*

The sun is just beginning to peek over the ocean horizon, casting a pinkish gold glow on them as they stand side by side

## The Crooner and The Comic

at the edge of the Boardwalk. Dean's big hands are curled around the railing as he watches the steady rise and fall of the tide in disbelief. Only the cool metal beneath his hands lets him know this is real. That everything that just happened was real.

Jerry can barely catch his breath as his mind works furiously to understand what happened. They had made it? Them? Him? Sure, Dean was always going to make it, it was just who he was, but Jerry? As much as he had wanted it, needed it, thirsted for it, there was always a part of him that doubted it was ever going to happen. But it did.

Only the rhythmic flapping of wings above them, the faint sizzling of the sand as the salty water creeps in and back, and the strong scent of the seashore stops Jerry from exploding. He feels like running, jumping, screaming. But he doesn't. He keeps it all inside. He just stands there alongside Dean, in silent acknowledgement of what has been and what is to come.

\* \* \*

Names: Dean Martin and Jerry Lewis

Year: 1946

Ages: 29 and 19

Over the mouthful of hot dog and mustard that drips messily from his lips, Jerry asks Dean, "Have ya seen our poster from 500?"

## Chapter Thirteen

"No." Is Dean's soft answer as he struggles to peel back the paper from his sandwich, tongue resting between his teeth in concentration.

"Well, I don't think the name is right. Lewis and Martin just isn't—it isn't any 'Abbott and Costello' or 'Laurel and Hardy', let's just say that." Jerry says while he racks his brain for a suitable alternative. He almost laughs out loud as he realizes what a pleasant problem it is to have. Just a little over a month ago he was wondering if he could afford his next meal without his *wife* sending him money. Now he was trying to find the right name for he and his partner's act. That's right. He has a partner now in an act that's getting him $750 a week.

"What about alphabetical order?" Dean finally asks, a satisfied expression on his face as he finally manages to peel back the paper—how he does anything like that with those paws of his, Jerry's not sure.

"Then we're back to Lewis and Martin."

"Not if you go by first names."

"Just 'Dean and Jerry?'" Jerry supposes that could work. It was a little unconventional perhaps, but it could work. Dean glances up from his sandwich just long enough to flash an annoyed look Jerry's way as he says, "No, idiot—'Martin and Lewis', but we use the first names, too, so it's 'Dean Martin and Jerry Lewis', and we make that contractual. We demand that it can't ever appear otherwise.'"

"Well, I guess—wait, but it was never 'Bud Abbott and Lou Costello', just 'Abbott and Costello', and for good reason, too."

"But they had alphabetical working both ways!" Dean retorts, and Jerry replies matter—of—factly, "Yeah, and L is before M."

"You wanna call this act 'Dean Lewis and Jerry Martin'?" Caught off guard, Jerry bursts out laughing.

77

*The Crooner and The Comic*

When he finally catches his breath, Jerry says, "Yeah, I guess you're right. 'Martin and Lewis' it is, then…I like it." Dean nods and goes back to eating, but Jerry gazes in contemplation at his partner. There was always something new to surprise Jerry about Dean . . . Every day his belief deepened that Dean wasn't who he tried to make himself out to be. That underneath that quick smile and even quicker fist is a heart bursting with feelings—sorrow, happiness, love, anger, confusion . . . Jerry just has to find a way to catch a glimpse into that heart.

## Chapter Fourteen

Names: Dean Martin and Jerry Lewis

Year: 1946

Ages: 29 and 19

Sweat clings to Dean's curls and covers his sun-kissed skin in a glistening sheen, and Jerry supposes he looks the same to the audience beneath the glaring spotlight illuminating them. The two stand so close to each other that to say "nose to nose" would have by no means been an exaggeration, and Jerry feels Dean's quick, warm breaths against the tip of his nose as he struggles to regain his own breath.

Dean's eyes are dark with something Jerry intimately recognizes as fury, and although usually he would have been quaking beneath that glare, Jerry can't help the smirk that tugs at the

*The Crooner and The Comic*

corner of his lips. He can't help the crazy ideas that pop into his mind, so he just has to follow this one and hope he doesn't end up on the ground with a bloody nose.

"I have finally come to the point in our relationship where I am going to have to tell you, if you do that again, it's *over*," Dean finally manages, his voice trembling with what only Jerry notices is real anger. The crowd eats it up, thinking this is all part of the act. "Do you understand that? O—V—U—R!"

Without letting himself think about it for one more second, for he knows otherwise he won't be able to bring himself to do it, Jerry leans forward and gives Dean a big kiss right on the mouth before saying, "I understand *perfectly*."

Despite the slight widening of his eyes, Dean just remains there, motionless. Apparently that was the right reaction, because the room erupts into pandemonium, and out of the corner of Jerry's eye he can see a few people in the front row actually falling out of their seats laughing.

They were going to be just fine.

\* \* \*

Names: Dean Martin and Jerry Lewis

Year: 1946

Ages: 29 and 19

"Why don't you knock off that crap and shut the hell up?" The group that are laughing at Jerry's jokes startle at the shout

## Chapter Fourteen

from the bar, and as soon as they catch sight of the perpetrator, they fall silent, paling. Jerry, unfortunately, does not note their expressions as due to the man in particular, and saunters over to the fella with his chest caved in and hips jutting out exaggeratedly. He gets these kind of drunks all the time, so he doesn't give joking around with him a second thought.

"That's what happens when cousins get married." The words escape in his squeaky Idiot voice, and he instantly regrets it when he glimpses the grimace on Dean's face. His stomach twists when the guy talking to Dean, Joe Lopez, shakes his head at Jerry and raises his fingers to his temple like a gun.

The supposed drunk moves to his feet, and Jerry swallows nervously. He certainly doesn't *look* drunk, and he certainly doesn't look like someone he'd want to get in a fight with, seeing as he seems to be a hulk of a man. With an expression that seriously makes Jerry wonder if he's about to be killed, the man sticks his finger in Jerry's face and growls, "That's not funny, you stupid sonofabitch. You open your mouth again, you won't have no teeth."

Jerry doesn't doubt it, and neither does Dean, who's muttering just about every curse known to man under his breath as he crosses the room in long strides. Nimbly stepping in between the hulking mountain and Jerry by pushing Jerry behind him, Dean turns on his charms to the max and says, "My partner's a little young, he didn't mean any harm." Jerry clutches at Dean's wrist almost instinctively as they watch to see the man's reaction, and in that moment in which all seems lost, his fingers dig into Dean's wrist so hard it would have been painful for Dean in any situation other than this.

"Okay. Only you keep the little bastard away from me. You tell him he's lucky I got a sense of humor." The man finally

### The Crooner and The Comic

says, throwing one last disdainful glare at Jerry before walking away. Jerry and Dean both sigh in relief, but the moment doesn't last very long as Dean whirls around to face Jerry with eyes flashing.

"For your information, schmuck, that was Albert Anastasia." Dean hisses, hating to admit to himself that he's only half angry, and that the rest of the adrenaline coursing through him is due to the fact that he's nearly scared out of his wits.

"Albert . . . Albert Anastasia?" The color drains from Jerry's cheeks as he puts two and two together. The guy that he very nearly drew to the edge was Albert Anastasia. A. K. A . The Lord High Executioner.

# Chapter Fifteen

Names: Dean Martin and Jerry Lewis

Year: 1946

Ages: 29 and 19

"Mmm." Jerry grins to Dean with the straw between his teeth as he sips the malted he just made, and from the bed Dean turns his head and crinkles his nose in disgust.
"How can you drink only a malted, day after day. With nothing else?" There is still a levity in Dean's eyes as he drawls that, and Jerry shrugs, sipping his drink to hide his smile.
"It tastes good." Jerry begins with his Idiot voice before breaking out his mock sophisticated voice with his lower jaw jutting out, "But you had better not do the same. Eat, my boy, build yourself up so you can continue to carry the Jew."

*The Crooner and The Comic*

"Hey, Jew. Shut it. I've gotta call Greshler." Dean lifts himself up in bed so his back is against a pillow on the headboard, and with drooped eyes he begins to call Abby. Jerry's heart pounds loudly in his chest with excitement, and he wonders how Dean doesn't feel the same way. They were about to close a major deal! This was *Hollywood* they were talking about! Hollywood! "Hey, Abby, what's the news?" From Dean's first words to Greshler, all Jerry hears for the longest time is the unintelligible sounds coming from Abby on the other end of the phone, and the occasional grunt from Dean.

Jerry slides down in his chair, arms flopped out over the sides, stomach twisting itself in knots. What was he saying? Did Mayer retract his offer? Were they taking the offer? Were they refusing it? God, why are they talking for so long! His eyes flit over to Dean, who is just lying there with one arm behind his head like he's at the beach. How can he be so cool and collected all the time? It always made Jerry feel like a freaking baby, but then again, he already knew that he was.

Even though Abby has already hung up, Dean milks the moment for all it's worth as he watches Jerry squirm from the corner of his eye. "Okay, Abby, I'll tell Jerry. He'll like that a lot." Upon putting the phone back, he slowly pats down his pockets for a cigarette and pulls one out, letting it hang loosely from his mouth.

Without even one glance Jerry's way, Dean swings his legs over the bed and walks around the entire hotel room in search for a match. Jerry feels like he might just burst any second, and exclaims, "Tell me already, you lousy fink! And use the goddamn lighter in your pants pocket." That expression of fatherly amusement Jerry's seen so many times crosses Dean's face, crinkling the corners of those chocolate eyes as he sits

## Chapter Fifteen

back down on the edge of the bed.

"Abby says he's not really interested in the Mayer meeting. He says we can do better."

\*\*\*

Names: Dean Martin and Jerry Lewis

Year: 1946

Ages: 29 and 19

"Jer! The Phone! It's your dad!" Dean calls out to Jerry, who's in the bathroom getting his hair done. If it was Dean's decision, he would chop all that hair off, cuz with all the orange-scented pomade the Kid manages to lather into his pompadour, Dean always feels like he's standing next to an orange tree.

The bathroom door bursts open, and Jerry is just a streak across the room until he ends up flopped on the bed, having torn the phone from Dean's hand. Shaking his head, Dean eases himself into an armchair in the corner of the room, watching Jerry with heavy-lidded eyes. The Kid's voice is unusually frantic, and Dean can tell that he's barely able to string together a coherent sentence as he asks with an excited expression, "Have you seen any of our shows?" His eyes widen. "Ya have?! Well, what did you think?!"

Dean's chest tightens as he watches the dark, flinty expression that enters the Kid's eyes. He can't hear what his dad said, but he can imagine. Dean's seen two reactions from the kid when it came to his parents, and it was usually in this order: happy, more happy than he would have thought anyone could be, and inconsolable.

Jerry's lying on his back now, free hand digging into the mattress as he fights to push back the emotions swirling within him that threaten to take over. But no, he can't give his dad the satisfaction. He would make it through the call with a curt goodbye, and then he could feel sorry for himself. He pushes all thoughts of the hurt aside and waits miserably for the end of the call. Matters are made worse when he catches sight of Dean watching him curiously as he slams the phone back onto its base, so he relegates himself to curling up on the bed, shoulders shuddering slightly as he tries to keep silent.

Why was he never good enough? Finally he was truly successful, really successful, and he still wasn't good enough for his dad. The realization makes him clench and unclench his fists in front of him. The tears come without his control.

Dean watches Jer's trembling form on the bed, and feels the corner of his own lips twitch. He hates being around someone else who's crying. It makes him want to go into another room, turn away and close his eyes and ears, anything but have to stay put, watching with this odd feeling inside and with nothing to do about it.

Finally he can't take it any longer; something inside of him is deeply disturbed at the sight of the Kid so silent and upset, and Dean moves over to the bed, clearing his throat so Jerry knows he's there. Jerry freezes for a second before turning his face towards Dean. There it is. That feeling again to leave the room, or hide, or something, but he forces himself to look at those red—rimmed, pleading eyes and that trembling lower lip. People often wonder how Jerry can play a Nine-Year-Old;

## Chapter Fifteen

Dean used to—but he knows now Jerry's not entirely playing.

"Germ . . . what is it? Anything . . .anything I can do?" Jerry can sense the strain in Dean's whisper, and sniffs back a sob as he tries to put into words what he's feeling.

"Naw—it's—it's just my dad. He never likes what I do." Dean feels a surge of anger, and feels like giving the Kid a pop in the mouth. If he went by what his parents said—what anyone else said, for that matter—he would still be in the steel mills. Or worse.

"He doesn't know what he's talking about, Jer. Listen to the guys paying us more than a grand a week. Not your dad."

"I don't know . . . it's not that easy." Jerry chokes out, not able to help the tears that roll down the side of his face into his hair. A shiver runs through him, and he abruptly shoots up and staggers off the bed so his back is towards Dean. What was he doing, crying in front of Dean? He was nearly 20 for goodness sake. Still a kid, Dean would say. Still a kid, many would say. Usually Jerry resented that word, but in this instance he would gladly take it.

He hears the bed springs groaning as Dean stands, and feels a warm hand on his shoulder. Jerry shuts his eyes for a moment, trying to quiet the panic and those terrible, terrible words that have been screaming at him. Then he turns into his Dean's arms and buries his face in his neck. Jerry gets a nose full of Woodhue, that cologne he likes so much because despite the camel hair coat and pimp shoes, and Luckies pack of cigarettes that all belong on the streets in New York, he can close his eyes and it's like they're standing underneath a canopy of pine trees.

Aware of the fact that Dean has stiffened beneath his embrace, Jerry lets himself have one more moment, with his

## The Crooner and The Comic

tears falling onto Dean's collar, before putting it all away. He'll get it back out tonight when he's in his own room. It's not too uncommon for him to lay there in the dark, panting for breath between the sobs that rack his body, fingers twisting in the blankets as he relives those moments that broke off a little piece of his heart here, another shard there.

Jerry's just about to pull back and laugh sheepishly as he quickly swipes at his cheeks with the backs of his hands when he feels Dean's shoulders drop slightly, and that big, warm hand of his comes in between Jerry's shoulder blades and stays there for a moment, telling him it's okay—he's okay. Then it drops, and Jerry knows that's all his partner can take for now.

**Later That Night**

"Tell me you love me, Momma." Jerry breathes into the mouthpiece of the phone. He's grateful for the night that engulfs his room so he doesn't have to be aware of the source of the wetness on his cheeks.

"I love you, Jerry." She croons, and he can just imagine her standing there in the kitchen beneath those bright lights, an amused smile on her face.

"Do you really? Why?" He's shrunk into the trembling, needy Kid with those words, and Patti knows it. But still she answers him with that same soft, reassuring voice, "Of course I do. You're my husband, and I wouldn't have married you if I didn't love you . . . Jerry, what happened today?"

"My dad called . . . He said my—" Jerry breaks off, sniffs back a sob. "He didn't like my performance. I just don't understand."

There's a pause on the other end, then a sigh.

"Jer, you know I respect your parents, and I know you do,

## Chapter Fifteen

but I've said this before and I mean it . . . Your dad wanted the success you're achieving, and he's jealous. I think you know that, too, because you are a wonderful performer, and there's no reason for his criticism otherwise." No. Jerry shakes his head although she can't see him, biting his lip hesitantly.

"No, I don't think that's it. I mean, he chose not to hit the big time so he could be there for me and my mom. He's not jealous." Those words make him feel no better, though, and Jerry has the unarticulated suspicion that Patti's right—but he can't think that of his dad. Musn't think that.

"Jerry, I've said all I can . . . I can't convince you about your dad, I just wish you'd stop beating yourself up over everything he says." With that, Jerry runs a hand over his face and exhales loudly before asking with a voice just a tad too cheerful, "How's everything with you and Gary?"

"Oh, they're fine." Patti responds, but her voice seems a little strained, a little distant. But Jerry can hardly blame her—raising a one year old boy practically by herself couldn't be easy. He feels a throb of guilt, but then his eyes widen in the dark and he exclaims, "Oh, Patti, I've got great news for you!! Guess what?!"

"What?"

"Greshler's giving me $110 a week now, so I can move you guys in with me!"

"Oh my goodness, that really is good news!" Patti's voice is genuinely excited now, and Jerry hears her sigh in relief. "That really is good news . . . I miss you, and I want Gary to be able to see his own father more often." Whether or not she meant it that way, Jerry feels the sting of accusation, and finds himself in defensive mode.

"I can't help being away from home, Patti. I've got to make

money, and this is the only way I can."

"I know, honey."

"I would love to see Gary everyday. You know that. You believe me, don't you?" He knows the answer, but he needs to hear it.

"I believe you."

"Good . . . " He relaxes his shoulders, not exactly sure why. "Well, I miss you, and I love you."

"I love you, too. Get some rest."

## Chapter Sixteen

Names: Dean Martin and Jerry Lewis

Year: 1947

Ages: 29 and 20

"Dean, they just don't get it. They just don't watch closely enough. Otherwise they would know that it only works if you have just the right timing—I mean, part of the time, *you're* the comic and *I'm* the straight man! There's no Martin and Lewis without Martin!" The words sort of tumble out of Jerry's mouth in a torrent, and he's half sorry he let them all out.

Dean crosses his legs and throws an arm behind Jerry on the park bench wordlessly, but a muscle jumps in his jaw. Jerry waits breathlessly for his reply, and finally Dean says dispassionately, "They don't know what they're talking about,

Kid. They don't watch."

"Yeah, but—"

"Who are ya tryna convince? There's no one here except you and me. I know it's crap and you know it's crap. End of story." Dean interrupts sternly, meeting Jerry's eyes with an unreadable expression.

Me. The word almost escapes Jerry's lips as he crosses his arms and lets his gaze return to the article. In reading their praises of him—his name was mentioned a ridiculous 12 times, and Dean's only ended up on the pages once—he felt a swell of pride, and it seemed as if he would never feel sad again, but he knows it isn't right. Dean's his partner, he should stick up for him. After all, Dean really was a vital part to the equation! You couldn't have just the putz. You needed the playboy and the putz, or the humor just wasn't there.

He sneaks a glance back up to Dean and frowns. How can Dean be so unaffected by this? If they did the same thing to him, well, let's just say they would never hear the end of it. A part of Jerry is jealous that Dean doesn't care—doesn't feel the sting of rejection—but another part of him doesn't understand how someone *couldn't* care! It was human nature.

Dean flicks away his cigarette as his stomach twists. He refuses to even think it could be from that stupid article; it's probably just that he's been smoking on an empty stomach. People were idiots who didn't care enough to actually watch closely and think. Newspeople just got paid to do it. Whatever. It doesn't matter at the end of the day; he knows what the truth is. With an inaudible sigh Dean squares his shoulders and shakes his head at himself, moving on to what he and Jerry would have for breakfast.

*Chapter Sixteen*

\* \* \*

Names: Dean Martin and Jerry Lewis

Year: 1947

Ages: 29 and 21

"Two very dry martinis, please." Dean tells the barkeeper, who does so while telling Dean and Jerry what a good job they did tonight. They say thank you politely and then sip their drinks in silence. That is, before the hairs on the back of Jerry's neck stand up on end and a big, meaty hand grabs him by the jacket. Jerry doesn't move as whoever is standing behind him turns him slowly, very slowly around as he sits on his revolving bar stool.

   At first Jerry glimpses the green, pyramid-shaped fez, the swaying yellow tassel, and he swallows. Oh, geez. This is the guy he made a joke about during the last show—he wished he had seen that this guy really wasn't one to mess with. But he just gets so focused in a show, he doesn't really think. His biggest vice.

   With dark eyes flashing, the man says slowly but menacingly nonetheless, "If I don't get an apology, I might knock you into next week." Jerry's mind races as he tries to come up with a good joke, or some way to get out of this without having to throw a punch. Because he would be the one coming away with a bloody nose. Or worse.

   Blinking in surprise, Jerry watches dumbly as Dean rises

## The Crooner and The Comic

silently from his seat, lips pinched together into one thin white line. As if in slow motion, Dean takes the man's hand from Jerry's jacket, puts a hand between the man's leg, and grabs his neck with the other hand. Then, with the strength of ten men, he throws the man into the shelf of glasses behind the bar. The ear-splitting crash and shattering of glass draw gasps from everyone around them, and for a moment the Lebanese man remains motionless on the floor in the midst of pools of liquor.

Jerry glances to Dean, breaking from his trance, and notes the heaving of his chest and the clenched fists. His own heart is thrumming like a hummingbird's wings . . . in fear . . . maybe in awe. He wants to thank Dean, wants to tell him how impressive that was, but he doesn't think he could form words—besides, he knows Dean would be embarrassed if Jerry mentioned it.

If he has to learn anything from this, it would be to not make Dean too mad at him.

**A Month Later**

Dean reads a line from his comic book. Forgets what he just read. Reads it again. Forgets it again. Throwing it aside, Dean takes a frustrated drag of his cigarette. He can't stop replaying the argument he just had with Jerry in his mind, anger boiling up inside of him as he does.

Who does Jerry think he is, talking to him like that? Dean's almost a decade older than him, for goodness' sake! A dull pain begins to throb in the back of Dean's head just as the phone starts ringing.

It's only been fifteen minutes since the argument; it better

## Chapter Sixteen

not be Jerry trying to yell some more at him.

"Hello?"

"I forgot to tell you . . . " It *is* Jerry. Dean prays Jerry won't say anything else to make him hate him. "I love you." With that, Jerry hangs up.

After the initial shock subsides, Dean puts the phone back with an incredulous shake of his head. This kid. Dean still wonders how on Earth Jerry's twenty years old. For Pete's sake, he's like a nine-year-old.

Dean wouldn't exactly describe himself as an 'I love you' type of guy. God knows he's only said that to his mom, Betty, Jeanne, and his kids. The same goes for other people saying that *to* him. But the Kid somehow gets away with it every time . . . Dean's been surprised countless times by him doing what Dean's other friends can sense they shouldn't do. But yet Dean lets him.

# Chapter Seventeen

Names: Dean Martin and Jerry Lewis

Year: 1947

Ages: 30 and 20

"Jer, I've made up my mind." Dean's voice is unusually serious for morning time as he throws the covers off and steps out of bed, exposing the fact that he's only wearing boxers—but then again, this *is* New York in the summer, and you can't exactly wear much more than that.

"Ya hafta make up your mind in the morning, like this? I've still got another hour before you have to bother me!" The bathroom door is cracked, and Jerry's voice comes back a little muted and distracted—no wonder, he's painstakingly doing his hair like he always does every morning. Jerry's hair. That

## Chapter Seventeen

goes back to what Dean's made up his mind about, and he stalks over to the bathroom and pushes the door open.

"I'm cutting your hair."

"Whaddya gotta cut my hair?" Jerry stops combing and eyes Dean suspiciously, shifting backwards slightly just in case Dean is planning on following through with what he said right then and there. Dean's about to tell Jerry he forgot the 'for', but if he's going to start correcting English, he'd be in a hell of a lot of trouble himself.

"I'm tired of always feeling like I'm working with a corpse, what with all the flies! Plus it's like someone rubbed oranges all over you, and then onto me!" Noting the determined glint that flashes in those dark eyes, Jerry knows there's no stopping Dean when he's convinced and fired up. But *he's* no doormat, either.

"I don't care! It's my hair, Dean . . . and besides, I've always had my hair like this! I like it!" Unable to help himself, Jerry squints his eyes and purses his lips in exaggerated indignation at Dean.

"Yeah, well I don't, and I'm not working with either the dead or an orange tree. The hair or me. You decide, pardner." Folding his arms, which Jerry note with jealousy are still two times bigger than his, Dean leans against the door frame.

"Alright, then, you win. I'll go to the barber first thing tomorrow." With that, Jerry turns back towards the mirror and begins carefully shaping his pompadour again. Dean snatches the comb out of his hand and says in a miffed voice, "No way I'm letting you wait until tomorrow! I'll just do it right now. I just *happen* to have a little experience cutting hair, if you so care to remember." Without hesitation, Dean grabs a pair of shears from his leather toiletry kit and tests them out. Yep.

*The Crooner and The Comic*

Sharp enough to easily make a mess of Jerry's ear with just one foul swoop.

"Oh no, you don't." Jerry tries to push past Dean, but of course it takes Dean little effort to grab him by the arm and swing him back in front of the mirror.

"Just stand still, Jer. I know what I'm doing." The humor has left Dean's voice as he immediately begins analyzing Jerry's hair like a real barber, and Jerry can see in the mirror the tip of Dean's tongue darting out from between his lips as he concentrates. As much as he would deny it to the moon and back, Jerry actually is pretty confident in Dean's barbering skills, and he wouldn't mind not having to spend an hour on his hair each day.

The first cut sends a shiver down Jerry's spine as the cold metal brushes against his scalp, and Dean immediately punches him angrily in the back.

"Ow! You give me a hit in the back like this, so hard?" Jerry cries out, and Dean shakes his head at him disapprovingly.

"You can't move while I'm doin' this, you're gonna get yourself cut!"

"You mean *you're* gonna cut *me!*"

"Same difference." Dean shrugs and returns his focus to Jerry's hair.

Finally, twenty long minutes later in which Jerry swears he can't feel his legs anymore, Dean steps away, like a proud artist admiring a painting. Jerry can hardly believe his eyes, and as he runs a hand over his head it feels foreign. Dean basically gave him a crew cut about a half inch from his scalp, and Jerry must admit that it's gonna do wonders for their act. It really makes him look a lot younger and more . . . monkey-like, and even makes Dean look taller than him.

## Chapter Seventeen

"At least we know you're not totally screwed if being a singer doesn't work out for ya."

\*  \*  \*

Names: Dean Martin and Jerry Lewis

Year: 1947

Ages: 30 and 20

"Dean." The word is barely more than a breath as they sit on chairs on opposite sides of the room, arms hanging over the sides and looking like they'd just finished a hard day of manual labor. It's 3 in the morning, and they've just finished their third show of the night—well, morning now.

"Shut up."

"I've got an idea, so get up." Jerry's voice is stronger now, and his eyes glint with excitement as he leaps off the chair with a sudden burst of energy. Dean slits his eyes open to glance at Jerry and then closes them again. No way was he going to get up. He can't even feel his legs anymore.

"Come on, Dean!! Get up, you lazy Italian!" Jerry's bony finger poking his chest leads to Dean opening his eyes in defeat. Once Jerry was up and at it, there was no stopping him. Rubbing the exhaustion from his eyes, Dean stands and follows Jerry into the center of the room.

"Alright, what's this crazy idea of yours?"

"Ya know how our act can be . . . well, physical?" Jerry asks

## The Crooner and The Comic

breathlessly, bouncing in place from foot to foot. Dean almost smiles at that. Physical isn't even a question when thinking of describing the countless times Jerry's flung himself onto Dean, or jumped on his neck, or done a hundred other crazy things. But that's all it is—Jerry doing crazy things. Dean's just stood there and taken it, all while throwing exasperated looks the audience's way.

"Yeah."

"Well, I think we should step it up a notch. I really think the audience would like it!" Dean's beginning to feel wary as to what idea Jerry has come up with, and says slowly, "How do you want to step it up a notch?"

"I want you should hurt me. Shove me back when I'm being annoying, throw me on the ground, whatever."

"I don't want to hurt you." Dean's taken aback, and is surprised at the sickening feeling that washes over him at the suggestion.

"No, you don't have to *actually* hurt me, Dean. We just have to make it look like you're hurting me."

"I'm not so sure." Dean looks down at his feet uncertainly. He thinks about the times anger has taken over him completely and he's sort of awoken from his haze having broken some guy's nose. He thinks about how he can circle his hand around Jerry's upper arm with room to spare.

"Oh . . . well, it was just an idea." The Kid's expression shifts, and he stops moving around in excitement. Shit. Dean hates it when he does that; when he can't just say the stupid thing he's thinking and he hurts the Kid like that.

"Alright. Fine, we'll try it. Just . . . if something happens, remember, you asked for it." Jerry nods eagerly and begins, "Great! You are *not* going to regret this," He moves over to

## Chapter Seventeen

Dean and faces him straight on. "Push me. Push me just about half as hard as you usually would."

"Then it won't look realistic!"

"Trust me. It will." Dean bites his lip hesitantly for a second before promptly pushing him in the chest. Jerry stumbles backwards and over a chair, ending up doing a sort of backwards somersault to land splayed out on the ground.

"Are you—"

"I'm fine, see? It's half me, half you, and it looks completely real!" Jerry springs up and bounds back to Dean, beaming and perfectly proud with himself. Dean doesn't like it, but he has to hand it to the Kid. It does bring up their act a step. As crazy as the Kid could be sometimes, as insecure and . . . afraid, Dean was continually surprised by how smart he was. It was like everything he tried he succeeded at.

They get so caught up with practicing, over and over again, with Dean pushing Jerry, pulling him, shoving him to the ground; and occasionally they get so rowdy that the people in the room next to them have to bang on their wall to get them to shut up.

## Chapter Eighteen

Names: Dean Martin and Jerry Lewis

Year: 1948

Ages: 30 and 21

"Paul, I hate you so much right now . . . we could have been up there five minutes ago, instead we have to climb fifteen flights of stairs." Jerry pants as they move slowly but surely up the stairwell, their uneven steps echoing like they're in a cave. Dean doesn't remember when Jerry started calling him Paul, matter of fact, he doesn't even remember telling him his middle name, but he doesn't mind. He suspects the Kid just wants a name that's his—everyone else calls Dean 'Dino', Betty calls him 'Dean'—so 'Paul' is his. The Kid was funny that way.

"I don't . . . like elevators, okay?" He manages, but is stopped

## Chapter Eighteen

by Jerry's hand flying out and grabbing him by the lapels of his jacket. Jerry's hazel eyes are wide and his face paling as he stares up at the man and woman making their way down the stairs their direction.

"Shit! It's my parents! Sorry, Paul, we've got to go in the elevator." With that, Jerry jerks Dean into the empty elevator behind them that just opened, and Dean's heart drops into his stomach as he watches those two doors block more and more of the world out. Then it's just him and Jerry in this small, godforsaken box—geez, when did elevators get so small—and it's moving now. Dean squeezes his eyes shut, tugs at his collar as the temperature rises several degrees within a few seconds, but his mind keeps conjuring images of the walls closing in, tighter and tighter until they're against him, pushing him, crushing him—His eyes fly open and he gasps out, but he realizes the walls aren't touching him, it's just Jerry's hand on his shoulder.

The Kid's looking at him with murky eyes, wondering if he's okay, confused at seeing him panic when usually Dean's the strong one, and it takes Dean a second to realize the doors have slid open already. Without a word, Dean strides out of the elevator and into the hall of apartments, taking in a deep lungful of the stale air of the apartment hallway, just grateful he's out of there.

\* \* \*

*The Crooner and The Comic*

Names: Dean Martin and Jerry Lewis

Year: 1948

Ages: 30 and 21

This was it. This could be the ticket to the big times, or the final performance for 'Martin and Lewis'. *You can do it. You're good enough. Funny enough.* The words are empty, though, as they echo through Jerry's mind, and for a moment he doesn't recognize the ringing of the telephone that has mingled with those words.

Reaching across the bed, he grabs the receiver, not really thinking about who it could be.

"Jerry? Jerry? What are you doing? Why haven't you come back or called me . . . or anything?!" Patti is nearly hysterical on the other end of the phone, and Jerry abruptly slams it back onto its base as his heart goes haywire. Blood pounds in Jerry's ears. It's all too much to feel, too much to think about.

The room's spinning, so he shuts his eyes, but it only makes things that much more insufferable. Thinking about Patti and Gary makes his chest tighten, thinking about their Copa debut makes him feel like he's about to be sick, and there's no escaping them in this darkness. His eyes fly open and he finds himself surging off the bed, throwing open the balcony doors with desperation.

The air is cool against his face, and he didn't realize how hot it was in the room. He stares out at the New York skyline,

## Chapter Eighteen

focusing on one particularly thin building that seems to come up to a point above the others, disappearing amongst the pink-tinged clouds. He just feels so . . . helpless. Like he has all of these things he's just *got* to do that he can't do. In this moment more than usual, Jerry wishes he had Dean's ability to throw every worry to the wayside. He wishes he had Dean here.

Dean picks up after three rings. "Yellow."

"Dean?" Oops, he didn't mean for his voice to come out like that, all high and . . . scared-sounding. He doesn't want to worry Dean, but he does want his attention.

"What is it, Jer?" Too late. The concern is apparent in Dean's voice, and Jerry can just imagine him sitting up from wherever he was lounging, stubbing his cigarette. "Jer? What's wrong? Did something happen?"

"No. I just—" He tries to explain, but he can't come up with anything. Finally he just says in a small voice, "Could you come over, Dean?"

"I'm on my way." Dean immediately says grimly, and the phone disconnects. For a few minutes Jerry tries to console himself with the knowledge that Dean's coming soon, but the thoughts just keep flooding back, like a dull headache that won't go away. So, Jerry hops off his bed again and hurries over to the cabinet where he keeps all of his drinks. He's not usually one who really drinks, he just doesn't like the feeling, but right now he wouldn't mind being a bit buzzed.

\* \* \*

Ten minutes ago, the only thing Dean wanted to do was lie in bed and watch a good Western. He didn't even want to *think* about getting up until tomorrow, he was so tired. But

## The Crooner and The Comic

when he heard Jerry's voice on the other end of the phone, his conscience pushed him out the door.

He had raced down the stairs and flagged down a cab to take him to Jerry's hotel suite. Fortunately Jerry's suite is on the first floor, so once he gets there he just has to go down the hall a little stretch.

He's just lifted his hand to rap on Jerry's door when he hears a crash, and he flings the door open, a dozen possible terrible situations flashing through his mind. What he finds was not one of them, but he's not exactly sure what to make of it. A tall lamp is on the floor, light bulb shattered, which is what made the noise, but what's odd is Jerry slowly raising himself up by leaning on the bed, not having even noticed Dean's entrance yet. Finally he's standing—well, swaying—and he catches sight of Dean.

"Dino, you're here!" He giggles and then lurches toward Dean, and seems more than once like his legs will give out on him, but he reaches Dean, and wraps his arms around him. Dean just stands there for a moment, totally dumbfounded, before shaking his head and dragging Jerry over to the bed. "What'reya doing?" Jerry slurs, and Dean turns his head with a loud exhale. His breath reeks of alcohol, and Dean can't believe it. He's never seen Jerry drunk.

Running a hand through his hair, Dean sighs to collect himself before swinging Jerry's legs onto the bed and undoing the first few buttons of his dress shirt. Jerry tries to bat his hand away, but Dean easily pushes his arm right back onto the bed. "Stop! Gerrof me, I'm alright. But . . . " Jerry is filled with a sudden burst of energy and sits up, eyes glossy but wide and looking at Dean. "I need your help. I dunno what's wrong with me." Jerry's eyes abruptly fill with tears, and he sniffs

## Chapter Eighteen

loudly.

"What's wrong, pal?" Dean chides, finding himself using the amused voice he reserves for his kids when they're sad about some silly thing.

"I'm not . . . I'm not living with Patti and Gary. My own wife and child. I don't know why, it's just they make me so—I can't." Jerry's voice breaks, and he stops for a second, just staring at Dean and swaying unsteadily where he sits. "I'm a terrible person, and beyond that, I'm gonna—gonna bomb at the Copa!"

"You're not a terrible person, Jer." Dean says, but an odd feeling washes over him. He feels . . . guilty. Geez, what the hell's he feeling guilty for? It's not like he *forced* the Kid to live by himself, or drink, or gamble, or go out with other broads. What was he kidding himself for? He knows the Kid doesn't need any more encouragement than to see him do something.

Swallowing, he gently pushes the Kid onto his back and says again, "You're not a terrible person, Jerry. And you're not gonna bomb at the Copa. You always do great."

"Yeah?" Jerry gazes up at him through heavy-lidded eyes, his fingers tugging on Dean's sleeve.

"Yeah." Dean can tell the hesitation in his voice, but Jerry's too out of it to notice. Jerry's fingers seem about to let go of Dean's jacket, and his eyes seem about to flutter closed, when his grip suddenly tightens and he gasps out in a small, slurred voice, "Then why do I feel so bad?"

Dean's throat constricts, and he looks down, gently pulling away Jerry's hand. He knows the Kid is always anxious about one thing or another, but . . . this time it's Dean's fault. He knows that if it weren't for him, the Kid would be like a puppy sticking by Patti's side and looking after his boy. But it can't be

*The Crooner and The Comic*

all his fault, right? I mean, after all, the Kid's just really nervous for the Copa, and he doesn't want the extra stress.

Taking a deep breath to control himself, Dean notices Jerry's shoes are still on, and with a soft tut-tut, he gently slides them off and tosses them onto the floor. Then, with one swift motion, Dean pulls the sheets over Jerry and says softly, "Just get some sleep, Kid."

"But Dean . . . " Jerry begins in a voice barely above a whisper, but he trails off as he drifts into unconsciousness. A soft sigh leaves Dean's lips, and he shakes his head. Damn it. He's going soft, and Dean Martin doesn't go soft. Not for anybody. Certainly not for some silly Jewish kid.

# Chapter Nineteen

Names: Dean Martin and Jerry Lewis

Year: 1948

Ages: 31 and 22

The door opens and shuts, and footsteps echo through the room as Dean approaches Jerry, but Jerry refuses to look up from his script. He's got to memorize this. The performance is tomorrow, for heaven's sake! To be fair, Jerry's probably got it down a hundred times better than Dean, but that isn't good enough. He's got to be able to do this in his sleep, and then some.

  He feels the couch shift from beneath him as Dean sits down beside him, but doesn't break his concentration from running his lines through his head.

## The Crooner and The Comic

"Jer, you don't want to read those lines, do you?" Dean says out of the blue, and Jerry blinks, looking at Dean over his script. Jerry went through all of the trouble to hire a writer, pay him $1,000, and spend every waking moment studying the material; and Dean's really going to ask him if he doesn't want to read the lines?

"No." He's a little surprised at how quickly the answer flies from his mouth, but when Jerry thinks about it, he really doesn't want to. It just doesn't seem wrong. After all, the magic between him and Dean didn't come about by prepared one-liners and gags. It just . . . happened.

"Then tear 'em up." A muscle in Dean's jaw jumps, and his eyes are narrowed slightly. He's serious! Heart doing somersaults in his chest, Jerry tears up his script, mixed feelings of panic and relief filling him.

\* \* \*

Oh God. The eager smiles on Patti's, his mom and dad's faces refuse to leave Jerry's mind, and he wonders miserably what he's going to do. He has no material, and they're here. They're sitting just outside in the audience, and they're going to see him fail, and they'll stare up at him with those blank expressions—or worse, in disappointment.

He shudders and takes a deep drag of his cigarette with trembling fingers as he strides back and forth in the small dressing room. A passing glance at himself in the mirror produces a harsh, nervous laugh from Jerry. Here he is, chainsmoking and pacing in his dressing room in only a dress shirt and boxers. What is he doing? He's just going to psych himself out, worrying like this.

## Chapter Nineteen

The muted sounds of the orchestra cease, and true silence fills his dressing room for a moment before thunderous applause can be heard even from where he is. His stomach flips as Jerry realizes what this means, and he thinks for one terrible moment he's going to be sick. When it passes, he hurriedly slips on his pants, and smushes the cigarette in an ashtray.

He meets Dean breathlessly half a minute later in the wings of the stage, and shoots a glance Dean's way. It doesn't give Jerry much solace that Dean looks as uncertain as he feels.

"Ya got a plan?" Dean whispers, eyes glued on the stage in front of them.

"Nope."

"Oy vey." The remark catches Jerry off guard, and he giggles, more out of nervousness than anything, and now it's time to go on stage.

Somehow Jerry makes his way to the mic, and risks a surveying glance of the audience. He recognizes Patti and his parents, Walter Winchell, and even Milton Berle, the latter two whose expressions don't exactly seem friendly. And why would they? It's not as if big shots like them came to see him and Dean!

Shutting his eyes for half a second, Jerry stops thinking. Stops worrying. Stops wondering. And just performs. When he opens his eyes and speaks, it comes out straight: "My father always said, 'When you play the Copa, son, you'll be playing to the cream of show business.'" He takes a moment to peer over the mic with squinted eyes, searching. Then, with Yiddish inflection, Jerry says, *"Dis is krim?"*

The laughter and applause that fills the room is to Jerry what water is to a man stranded in the Desert. It looked like this was going to be their ticket to the big times, after all.

## The Crooner and The Comic

\* \* \*

Names: Dean Martin and Jerry Lewis

Year: 1948

Ages: 31 and 22

Dean gazes up at the ceiling through the dark, just thinking. Thinking about Jerry onstage by himself, more anxious than anyone would have thought possible, but still delivering a riotous show. Thinking about the anger—and fear— in Jerry's eyes as he yelled at Dean about Jeannie. *She's with you all the time,* Jerry argued. *I don't like it,* he said . . . then finally: *Her or me, buddy.* So, Jerry's on alone tonight.

He turns under the sheets onto his side, propping his head with his arm on his pillow. Jeanne is fast asleep facing him, her strikingly blond hair pinned up behind her head. With her perfect hourglass figure, elegant features, and lovely dovetail lips, Jeanne's like a doll. A cute, real-life doll. He thinks of Betty, and frowns in the dark. But he only thinks of Betty for a moment, because Jeanne dominates his thoughts.

The phone rings, startling him for a second, and he clicks on the lamp on his side of the bed. He knows who's calling. He doesn't want to answer it—he knows what's going to happen. But he answers it anyway.

"Hi, Jer." Defeat resounds in those words, and Dean runs a hand over his tired face.

"Please come back, Paul. It's awful lonesome without you."

## Chapter Nineteen

Jerry whines in his Idiot voice. Why can't he just be serious for once? But Dean knows deep down that's not the issue. Jerry uses the Idiot persona as a mask; a defense. He pretends to be someone else so nobody can reject the real Jerry. Dean doesn't say anything when he himself is hurting.

Dean exhales softly through gritted teeth. He's already in bed. He's with Jeanne. He's still mad at Jerry—ah, what's he kidding himself for. He can just imagine Jerry on the other end, hoping. Worrying so much he's forgotten to breathe. Always worrying something's going to go wrong, and if something's already wrong, he's worried he won't be able to fix it.

"Okay." When he hangs up and turns back to Jeanne, he finds she's sitting up in bed, gazing at him with a kind of sad expression on her perfect face.

"Are you going back to him?" Dean nods, catching the disappointment that flickers through her eyes. For a moment Dean muses over how similar this feels to when he was with Betty. The only difference is, he tries harder with Jerry than he did when he was with Betty.

\* \* \*

Is he gonna show up? Please, God, let Dean show up. Jerry tries to remind himself Dean said he would. But he wouldn't put it past Dean—the fella sure has a funny way of being mad. He'd sooner drop off the face of the planet where his offender is concerned than actually confront him.

He checks his watch. Only ten minutes until showtime. His heart does somersaults in his chest as the prospect of going on alone again. The audience didn't pay just to see *Lewis*. They wanted to see *Martin and Lewis*.

## The Crooner and The Comic

The dressing room door abruptly swings open, stopping Jerry in the tracks of his pacing.

"Hi, pallie. How'd you do without me?" Dean offers him a small smile of unspoken forgiveness. Telling him things are okay between them.

Jerry wants so badly to cross the room in two strides and bury his face in Dean's neck; to hide his shame and fear even from himself—all of which seem so silly now that Dean's here. But he settles for just returning Dean's smile and murmuring, "Not too good, Paul. I don't think the Jew's ready to be alone."

## Chapter Twenty

Names: Dean Martin and Jerry Lewis

Year: 1948

Ages: 31 and 22

As soon as Dean walks into the room, he can sense something is wrong. Jerry is lying fully-clothed on the bed, staring up at the ceiling unblinkingly, not even acknowledging Dean entering the room. The silence is unnerving for Dean, as usually the Kid is practically begging for his attention the moment he sees him—like he's been waiting for hours to talk to Dean.

Dean crosses the room and stands at the window with his back to Jerry, waiting for him to say something or sneak up and jump on his neck—do anything. A minute passes, and it seems like far longer as discomfort hangs in the air; usually

## The Crooner and The Comic

Dean hopes for silence more than anything... Not this time. He opens his mouth to say something, he's not sure what yet, he's saved from figuring it out when Jerry abruptly says, "I cheated on Patti."

Shock makes the hairs on Dean's arms stand on end, but he keeps his face level when he turns to Jerry. Staying on his back, Jerry's eyes flit down to Dean, clouded with confusion, maybe guilt.

"Oh." Is all Dean says, and he knows he doesn't have to ask for Jerry to tell him the story.

"I just went out with this girl who was at our show last night, and... I don't know... it just sorta happened. But... well, *you* do it all the time!" Jerry exclaims, flustered, and when Dean doesn't respond, he hurriedly adds, "Not that it's your fault, Paul, I wasn't saying that, I just—well, people like us do that all the time, right?"

Dean can see the pleading in his eyes, and knows that Jerry just wants to hear that it's okay. Who was he to say the Kid was wrong, anyhow? Although *Dean* certainly could care less who went out with who, he feels... guilty. Aduzipach! But that's crazy! The Kid's full grown, he can make his own damn decisions. If he wants to imitate Dean, then let him! He ignores the voice that says Jerry idolizes him, that the Kid would do anything he did without question—isn't that Dean's responsibility then?

"You can do what you want, Jer... I'm not you... You love Patti, right?" The Kid nods desperately.

"Well, I love Betty and my kids, and what I do away from home is my business—I don't bring it home with me, and it doesn't hurt them." Dean slowly says, shifting in his shoes uncomfortably. "You shouldn't feel like you have to do

## Chapter Twenty

anything, but don't let anyone tell me you can't do something, either. Do what makes you happy coz you're the one who has to live your life, nobody else . . . Yeah." Dean shrugs his shoulders, satisfied with his explanation.

Jerry looks back up at the ceiling, tapping the mattress restlessly with his fingers. Yeah, that makes sense. He loves Patti. He's happy this way, so what's wrong with that? He fights to dissipate the guilt eating at the edges of his mind, curling his lips into a perpetual frown.

Finally he rationalizes it out, and sits up, a somewhat forced smile plastered on his face.

"Thanks, Dean, that really helped."

"Sure, kid." Dean's voice is softer than normal—was that uneasiness Jerry sensed? He couldn't be judging him, that was for sure. Oh, well, he was sure Dean just didn't care.

\* \* \*

Names: Dean Martin and Jerry Lewis

Year: 1948

Ages: 31 and 22

Jerry can't help the persistent grin on his face. He has always imagined what it would be like to sit in a canvas director's chair—one with his name on it would be a dream come true. He has always imagined what it would be like there on set, behind the scenes where you can see all the

## The Crooner and The Comic

cameras, all the lights, all the people bustling around getting the props and people ready. He has always imagined what it would be like to meet someone like Stan Laurel or Rudolph Valentino—someone who he can hardly believe exists in real life.

Now he's here, and doesn't have to imagine. The chair is a little stiff, but makes him feel important nonetheless—not just another guy off the street or a wannabe anymore, but a someone. Oddly enough, seeing the set in its entirety doesn't disillusion the movies he's seen and loved. If anything, it captures him, makes him so curious as to how they make something like this seem so real . . . so significant and valuable on screen. As for meeting an actor, he doesn't quite get to see Rudy, but when Marie Wilson and Diana Lynn come waltzing onto the set like this is just another day in the life, which it is for them, Jerry and Dean shoot up from their seats, smoothing out their suits in starstruck nervousness.

It isn't even that they particularly fancy Marie or Diana, but it's just mind-boggling to see them standing there—where Jerry and Dean can touch them, smell them, talk to them. The pictures haven't done justice to Diana, they note—she's gorgeous. The director, Mr. Marshall, introduces them all rather matter-of-factly, and Dean manages to keep his cool despite the fog that has settled over his mind of disbelief, and Jerry somehow manages not to lapse into his Idiot voice even once.

\* \* \*

Dean's first screen-test with Diana brings a smattering of shocked applause from the crew, as they never expected him

## Chapter Twenty

to look so good on screen the very first time, and Jerry feels a swell of pride—and hope that this whole movie thing really will work out. Then they're off to lunch before Jerry's screen test, and as usual Dean heaps up a full two meals onto his tray, while Jerry can hardly look at the food because of the fluttering in his stomach.

As they eat—well, as Dean eats—they catch sight of people heading into the Private Dining Room reserved for box-office hit actors, and feel lightheaded as they spot Gary Cooper, Burt Lancaster, and Rosemary Clooney among them. Jerry has a general reverence for all of them, but Dean is focused on one person in particular: Bing Crosby. He watches slack-jawed as those droopy, crystal blue eyes survey the room, landing only for a split-second on the handsome Italian and the monkey-like Jew beside him.

\* \* \*

The screen finally goes black, and Jerry feels like slinking away in the dark of the screening room while he can, or at least keeping his eyes closed forever so he doesn't have to see their expressions. He honestly did not foresee himself totally bombing his screen test.

Unfortunately, though, the lights flick back on, and the twenty or so men sitting around the table are wearing one expression: disappointment. Finally Hal Wallis says slowly, like he's picking his words carefully, "I think we must move ahead with great care, given the very significant commitment we've made to Paramount on Martin and Lewis. We have to deliver on that commitment. Now, my suggestion is that we all sleep on this, and reconvene at the end of the workday

## The Crooner and The Comic

tomorrow to begin to formulate a plan."

Jerry feels a surge of anger—he knows what they're all thinking! They want to somehow keep Dean and leave him to hang in the wind! Not that he could exactly blame them after watching his screen test, but it somehow wasn't fair! Dean's not an actor! Jerry's been working practically his whole life on entertaining and performing, and he knows he can be a good actor.

Swallowing his anger, Jerry stands along with everyone else at the conclusion of the meeting and moves to leave, noting that only Dean would look him in the eye. Even then, Dean's expression is grim at best.

As Jerry and Dean sit sullenly in their suite, the room may be silent, but their minds are practically shouting at them. Jerry's trying to justify to himself why he did so badly—after all, that Al character was nothing like who he was in the nightclubs with Dean! It was like hiring on a farmer expecting him to be an accountant!

Dean's trying to decide what to do. He's sharp, despite all of the contrary messages his exterior might deliver, and he knows just as well as Jerry what the executives were trying to say. At the end of the day, sure he wants to become a movie star and all of that other crap, but not nearly as much as the kid—the kid *needs* this. Dean doesn't have many rules he forces himself to live by; many codes, but loyalty is one.

"Hey, who the hell wants to live in Los Angeles, anyway?" Dean finally says, and Jerry turns to look at him with clouded eyes. He knows what Dean's about to say, but he's not sure if he wants to hear it. "Listen," Dean continues. "If they just put the camera on what we did at the Copa, it would've been great!"

## Chapter Twenty

"But that's not what movies are about. Movies are about personalities playing characters. Movies are about story." Jerry responds, a note of bitterness in his voice.

"Well, I say bullshit . . . I say it's Martin and Lewis or nothing." Dean stares at Jerry brazenly, and Jerry knows without a doubt that he means it. But Jerry's torn. On one side, he's relieved Dean won't let him fall to the wayside without a fight—he's also a little surprised, to be honest, that Dean cares enough. But on the other hand, he's not gonna let Dean throw away what could be his only chance at stardom for him.

# Chapter Twenty-One

Names: Dean Martin and Jerry Lewis

Year: 1948

Ages: 31 and 22

Learning lines. Waiting three hours. Shooting a scene for thirty minutes. Learning more lines and waiting around another few hours. Although it's only been like this two months, Dean can't remember what it was like before this.

As soon as he's inside, Dean slumps into his favorite armchair and tosses his keys onto the coffee table. Shutting his eyes that are beginning to hurt from being open too long, he folds his arms across his chest and sighs. He's just going to rest for a little while here and then go to bed . . .

"Daddy?" He hears Craig's whisper, which really isn't much

## Chapter Twenty-One

quieter than his normal voice, and feels small hands tugging at his trousers as Craig pulls himself onto Dean's lap. Dean wants to keep his eyes closed, wants so desperately to sleep, but when Craig says, "Daddy, I'm hungry," Dean sits up and opens his eyes in dismay.

Craig is sitting precariously on his lap, big dark eyes wide and staring up at Dean expectantly.

"Craig…did momma not get you and your sisters dinner?" Dean cups Craig's small chin in his palm and searches his eyes real closely—although seeming unwilling, Craig nods and whispers, "Or lunch."

Damn it, Betty. This is the third time this week. Now wide awake, Dean lets out a loud breath and cracks a smile—if kids see you smile, then nothing's wrong.

Scooping Craig off his lap and setting him back onto the ground, Dean runs a hand through Craig's dark locks and sends him to tell his sisters daddy's going to make fried-egg sandwiches.

Calm, still, peaceful sleep would just have to wait…

*  *  *

### The Crooner and The Comic

Names: Dean Martin and Jerry Lewis

Year: 1948

Ages: 31 and 22

A blond curl shimmering in the sun. Two eyes, blue as can be, all but disappearing as the face breaks into a smile. Two girls stepping out of a limo in mink stoles and dresses that make it impossible for Jerry and Dean not to notice their perfect hourglass figures.

As they stop in the lobby, Dean and Jerry finally approach them, amazed all over again at how beautiful they are—and how small they are—the two girls lift their heads practically all the way just to look them in the eyes.

"Hi, June. Are you two staying here, darling?" Dean wastes no time in greeting June Allyson, the girl with blond locks and a wide, innocent smile. *Ma che bell'!* Jerry notes with a pang of jealousy that she blushes as soon as she recognizes Dean—they always do—before turning to her friend Gloria, whose thickly lashed sky blue eyes and full, pouty lips aren't exactly those of the girl-next-door.

Dean and Jerry exchange a knowing glance when they find out the actresses are sharing a suite on the 25th floor—Dean's is on the 23rd, and Jerry's is on the 24th. The next four days are history.

\* \* \*

## Chapter Twenty-One

No, not yet. Jerry slits his eyes open just enough to see the faint, pinkish light of dawn that streams through the blinds of the suite, and he can make out the figure of Dean sitting on the edge of the bed with his face in his hands.

The phone sounds like a jackhammer in the middle of Jerry's brain, and he slams it back on its base with fingers still weak from sleep just so it would stop ringing.

"Hey, Jer, this is important." Somehow Jerry notices that Dean sounds serious—a little shaken, perhaps.

"What time is it?" The words come out hoarsely from Jerry.

"It's four A.M., and I just had a great hour on the phone with Betty!" Oh boy. Jerry knows he won't be able to get out of this one, and he begrudgingly rubs the sleep from his eyes.

"Maybe we better cut back a little. There are more eyes on us than I ever could've imagined." Dean mutters, bringing the cigarette to his lips again and again in a state of nervousness Jerry doesn't remember seeing on him more than once. Jerry's too nervous for himself to think about the full implication of what Dean just said.

Two hours later Jerry slams the phone back onto its base, mind reeling. At the end of the day, Patti hadn't been angry at the fact that he had gone out with Gloria, she told him she expected it from a man in his business, but she was just not going to tolerate him humiliating her. Jerry knew she was right, and did his best to appease her on the phone .

He ignores the lurking thought that he's broken Patti's trust. That he might hurt Gary. *Dean* doesn't seem to worry about that. And Dean would know.

\* \* \*

## The Crooner and The Comic

He and Dean, however, had not heard the last of their gallivanting. The very same day they find themselves cornered by their public-relation agents, George Evans and Jack Keller. As soon as George begins to speak, Jerry is hit once again with what Dean realized early that morning.

"Do you guys realize that your anonymity is gone? That you are now public property?" George says, and Jerry winces at that last word—he doesn't see it, but so does Dean. "That you cannot do whatever you want anymore? Don't you realize that you, you Italian idiot, are married with three children, *and* you're Catholic? Which is just a tad more serious than it is for the Jew with the one kid? Your people still go to confession!" Jerry half-expects Dean to lunge across the table and punch George square in the mouth. But Dean just looks at the floor, chewing his upper lip. When Jerry finally manages to catch Dean's eye, he knows what they're both thinking: this is their life now. Like it or not, this is their life—this is the life they asked for, and this is the life they've got now.

## Chapter Twenty-Two

Names: Dean Martin and Jerry Lewis

Year: 1948

Ages: 31 and 22

Of course it had taken until Dean was in bed, stripped to his boxers, favorite comic book already opened to the right page, for him to realize his glasses are in Jerry's room. How did he even leave them anywhere other than their usual hiding place beneath his socks? Dean exhales loudly in frustration. Whatever the reason, he's been looking forward to reading this issue of Tom Mix all day, and he needs his glasses.

After procrastinating for five more minutes, Dean finally flings off his covers and sits up, flinching at the cool gust of air that sends goosebumps slithering up his arms and legs. He crosses the bedroom in a few long strides and opens the door to the hallway, where Jerry's door is about a foot from his. Using the spare key, Dean slowly, quietly eases Jerry's door open, careful not to open it enough to catch Jerry's bed with the light filtering in from the hallway. Once the door is closed, engulfing the room once again in darkness, Dean takes careful steps forward, having snuck into a room undetected more than once in his day.

He can tell he's almost to the dresser where he's sure he left his glasses when one of the legs of the bed catches his toe, and he can't help the hiss of pain that leaves his lips. Almost immediately after, Dean hears a rustle coming from the bed and an eerily recognizable metallic click that Dean desperately hopes is not what he thinks it is.

"Don't move, whoever you are. I've got a gun." Jerry's voice comes out all squeaky at first, but then his normal voice leaks through, trembling as it does. Holy crap. The Kid's got a gun. Since when did the Kid get a gun?

Somehow Dean manages to choke out, "Woah, Jer! It's just me!" But there's no sign of movement, so Dean moves forward, fumbling until he finds the switch on the lamp. Light floods the room, illuminating a wide-eyed, trembling Jerry with pistol at his side. "Put the gun down so you don't shoot yourself in the foot." Dean says softly, gently prying the gun from Jerry's fingers. His heart doesn't slow until he's sure the gun is pointing away from any part of him.

"I'm sorry, Paul." Jerry abruptly breaks from his trance and hurriedly climbs over the bed to stand a foot or so away from Dean with his back facing him. Still in disbelief, Dean looks at the gun in his hand. It's obviously an expensive pistol, not at all

## Chapter Twenty-Two

like the cheap ones he was used to seeing growing up. He takes out the magazine and shakes his head. So the gun really was loaded. That could have gone very, very badly. Dean quickly empties the bullets into the first drawer of the nightstand and places the parts of the gun in there beside them.

The barely audible chattering of teeth averts Dean's attention back to Jerry, and he sympathetically reaches out to put his hand on Jerry's bony shoulder. Jerry immediately flinches away and goes into the bathroom, not once facing him. Dean hears water running in the sink, but can only see a line of white light from the cracked door.

Running a hand through his hair, Dean struggles with whether or not he should try to talk to him, or leave him alone. Well, he knows the Kid doesn't do well alone when he's upset. Besides, as much as he wants him to cool off, he's dying to know why he has a gun—he's probably been keeping it under his pillow, too.

With an audible sigh, Dean heads over to the bathroom and slowly pushes the door open all the way. Jerry is leaning over the sink, water dripping from his hair and the tip of his nose, having just splashed his face with water. Clearing his throat awkwardly, Dean says, "Sorry if I scared you, Jer. I was just trying to get my gla—something, and I didn't wanna wake you." Jerry swallows and glances up at Dean for a second, but says nothing, and quickly returns his hardened gaze to the water slowly draining at the bottom of the sink.

What's this? For as long as they've known each other, the Kid has always been an unstoppable spew of words, only shutting up if Dean buys him a malted or threatens to cave his face in with his fist. But now . . . nothing? "Jerry, you almost gave me a new nose." He jokes, expecting to get a laugh, or at least a

## The Crooner and The Comic

comeback, but Jerry's white-knuckle grip on the sides of the sink just tightens.

Dean's heart sinks, and he says again, a little more forcefully, "I really am sorry, Jer. I didn't mean to scare ya." Finally, after another long moment of silence, Jerry unexpectedly chuckles and says, "*You're* apologizing to *me*? I'm the one who drew a damn gun at you!"

Dean grins, relieved, but notices the slight trembling in Jerry's hands as they clutch the sink, and says seriously, "Are you sure you're fine?"

"Yeah, just a little freaked, that's all. It's my own fault, though."

"You know we've got security."

"I know."

"So, what are you doing with it under your pillow?"

"Nothin'. I've gotta right. It's not hurting nobody."

"Except me. You almost shot me, Jer. That can't be safe." Jerry lowers his gaze guitily and shrugs.

"Sorry." Sorry? Why does the Kid keep apologizing? Dean's more worried about him than himself at this point. Jerry's paranoia has gone up just about a hundred notches, and that can't be good for anybody.

"Listen, Jer. No one even knows we're here, and besides, the clerk's not gonna just let anybody up to our rooms. If it makes you feel better, we can have more police stationed somewhere outside. Just . . . don't sleep with a gun."

"Why?"

"It'll make me feel better knowing you won't shoot me, and you won't accidentally shoot yourself!"

"Okay. When we're on the road together, I'll try not to sleep with it. Satisfied?" Jerry looks up at Dean with mock annoyance. Dean shakes his head with a hint of a grin before placing his hand on Jerry's shoulder and saying softly—almost bashfully, "And Jer, you know I'll always . . . well I'll always take care of anyone tryna hurt you."

A playful glint passes through Jerry's eyes, and before Dean can say another word, Jerry has leaned forward and kissed Dean on the cheek.

\* \* \*

Names: Dean Martin and Jerry Lewis

Year: 1948

Ages: 31 and 22

The atmosphere surrounding Dean and Jerry in the room is exciting and overwhelming—so many lights, so many people, so many shouts—it's intoxicating. As Dean's gaze sweeps the crowd, not really looking, but in his own head because that's the only way he can focus on the song, one pair of eyes drowns out everything. It's like someone suddenly turns down the volume on a radio, and Dean stares at the girl unblinkingly for what seems like minutes, but is only seconds.

Dean can hardly wait to finish the song; he wants to hop off the stage right then and there and find her. He doesn't have to wait very long, though, and wades through the crowd to head over to her ringside table. Jerry watches him disappear amongst the audience in amusement. Little does he know what an impact this girl would make in his partner's life. He didn't think a broad *could*.

\* \* \*

"I know your type." Jeanne says as they walk along the shoreline, wind billowing her dress behind her like scarlet smoke. Dean glances sideways at her, but she's smiling ahead, blue eyes sparkling knowingly.

"What's that?"

"You know exactly what to say, and you say it to every girl who catches your eye."

"Can you blame me?"

"No," Jeanne finally says, a pensive expression on her practically perfect face. "Why do you act this way? I mean, you act like you don't care about anyone, and you go out with all of these girls. Why?" With pursed lips, Dean begins shedding his suit, and slips off his shoes before holding out a hand to Jeanne with a playful grin.

"Would you care for a midnight swim?" For a moment Jeanne looks like she's going to be upset at Dean, but then her expression shifts and her hand disappears in his.

## Chapter Twenty-Three

Names: Dean Martin and Jerry Lewis

Year: 1949

Ages: 31 and 22

"What the hell, Dean?!" Before the front door even shuts behind him, Betty's shout pierces him, sending his heart racing as he thinks about everything he could have done that she could be angry about. It's an extensive list.

With soft steps, Dean hesitantly rounds the corner into the kitchen, and as soon as he catches sight of the basket of oranges, his heart drops. *Jeanne.*

"Do you have something to tell me?" Betty demands, face flushed and hands trembling slightly. It doesn't take Dean long

## The Crooner and The Comic

to guess that she's been drinking.

"Have an orange." He picks one up out of the box and holds it out to her. She doesn't have a leg to stand on; he is a pretty famous guy, after all. "They're good." She smacks it out of Dean's hand, eyes darkening.

"Read the tag. I'm not stupid, Dean." Mouth going dry, Dean glances at the tag attached to the crate out of the corner of his eye, and sees the cursive, flowery letters. For the first time, Dean finds himself unable to say anything, unable to defend himself. "I know you go out with other girls, Dean. You're an attractive man and you've always had girls throw themselves at you. I know. But you can't do this. She's sending things to *our house*! The kids live here, Dean! *I* live here! Who is she? Do you even love her? What can she give you that I can't?!" Betty's cries fall on deaf ears, and Dean looks down at his shoes before saying softly, "I should go, Betty. This isn't making me happy, and I'm sure not making you happy. You don't deserve to be hurt by me. We've had four beautiful children together, and—"

"No, Dean! You can't say that! You can't give up on us! Remember your children! They can't have their father leave!" Betty desperately grabs the sleeve of Dean's jacket, her final attempt at communicating something that can only be felt. He places a big hand on hers and gently pulls her fingers from his sleeve, before leaning forward to kiss her forehead.

"I'm sorry."

### Two Days Later

"Hey, Paul?" Jerry's voice seems far away, and Dean doesn't feel like answering.

## Chapter Twenty-Three

"Paul?" Dean's eyes remain glued to something outside the window, and Jerry frowns before trying again, but this time he grins mischievously and uses a slightly higher, more feminine voice like he does sometimes in their act: "Deanie?" Finally Dean blinks back the moisture in his eyes and turns his head to face Jerry.

"Sorry, Kid. I was just thinkin'. What's buggin' you?" Dean still sounds a little bit distracted, but he's obviously making an effort to focus.

"Well, I've noticed you've been a little bit down lately, so I, uh . . . " Jerry glances down, abruptly bashful. "I got ya somethin'. Nothing big, just thought it would make you happy." With that, Jerry reaches behind the couch he's sitting on and pulls up a brand new golf club with a little green bow messily tied around the handle.

A wide smile breaks onto Dean's face, and he shakes his head as he takes the club.

"Ya didn't have to do that, Jer. Thanks a lot." Jerry's practically beaming as he points excitedly to the area just beneath the rubber handle and says, "And see? I have a little something written there." Dean glances to where he's pointing and reads the words etched into the metal: *LOVE, THE JEW*. He finds himself grinning as he stares down at the words, but then a wave of coldness washes over him. He's no good. Just like he hurt Betty and his kids, he's bound to hurt the Kid sometime. Here he is, never having given the Kid anything bigger than someone to talk to—who wouldn't necessarily talk back, and the Kid spends all this money on him with nice things written trying to make him feel better.

"Thanks, Jer . . . I'm gonna go see what westerns are on now." Dean mumbles, rising from his seat and leaning the club against the wall, but as he turns to go to the other room, he catches sight of Jerry's face falling in disappointment. Dean hates himself for it, but he purses his lips and whispers just loud enough for Jerry to hear, "You want I should watch by myself?" Almost as if on cue, the Kid's face brightens, and he leaps up to follow Dean into the other room.

\* \* \*

Names: Dean Martin and Jerry Lewis

Year: 1949

Ages: 31 and 23

Red. What a color. That brilliant, blinding scarlet takes up all of Jerry's vision, and the breath hitches in his throat as his mind blanks on the next joke. Dean senses something is wrong before Jerry has to glance at him in desperation, and Dean kindly makes up a reason for going into another song.

Jerry forces his legs to move as he stumbles off the stage, heart racing in his chest as he curses himself for messing up over some broad. But as soon as he's in the wings, invisible from the audience, he can't help looking over to see if she's still there. Yep. That flaming dress, those wild blond curls, those piercing eyes—man, he wants to see what color those eyes really are.

It takes him another awed second of staring to realize that she's smiling up at Dean, and he's singing solely to her. Shit.

## Chapter Twenty-Three

Why would she want the monkey when she could have a whole god?

But his awe immediately disappears when he realizes he's not the only one who has noticed the connection between her and Dean. A rather disgruntled-looking man beside her who seems to be her boyfriend is glaring at Dean so furiously Jerry's surprised there isn't fire coming from his eyes.

Jerry continues the rest of the show, forgetting about the girl until he walks into the restroom afterwards. He can hardly believe the sight that beholds him, and his heart drops like a stone. That broad's boyfriend is standing less than a foot from Dean, jabbing a .38 into Dean's stomach. An image instantly pops into Jerry's mind of Dean slumped on the bathroom floor, clutching at the scarlet that blossoms across his shirt, and when he somehow focuses enough to look at the man's face, he realizes that was more than likely to be a reality. The guy pointing the gun was a low-level hood who would not have a problem in the world with knocking off someone who was flirting with his girlfriend.

Before giving terror the chance to grip him and render him completely useless to Dean, Jerry steps in between his partner and the gun, the cold metal sending goosebumps crawling up his arms and legs.

Jerry makes a quick calculation and says as convincingly as he can despite the hammering in his heart, "Listen, you have to understand something. People make mistakes—that's why they have erasers on pencils. Now, I'm going to admit to you that my partner made a mistake. I know Dean did what you said he did, but I'm going to offer you my hand, to give you my word of honor that I know my partner, and I know that out of respect for you, out of the same respect I have for you, he would never have done this if he had known who this young lady was."

With that, he extends his hand and watches breathlessly for a reaction. The man's dark, narrowed eyes flit from Jerry's hand to his gun, and back to Jerry. Another painful moment passes, and then the man puts his pistol back into his waistband. Jerry exhales in relief.

"This one time. This one time. But if he *ever*—"

"He will never," Jerry hastily interrupts.

"Ever," The man repeats.

"Won't happen," Jerry swears—he doesn't care if it's a lie, he just wants to live. The man stares down Dean until he's satisfied they're telling the truth, and then he stalks out of the men's room as if nothing happened.

Jerry was so preoccupied with disarming the situation he didn't get a good look at Dean, but now it's just him and Dean staring at each other wide eyes, and now Jerry knows what *he* must look like. Dean's got the hem of his coat clutched in a white—knuckled grip, and a sheen of sweat covers his colorless face. The silence that's descended upon them is thick and hot; Jerry feels like he's going to choke on it. That or break into tears.

Finally Dean breaks the silence and says with a voice just slightly louder than necessary, "I've never seen a more stupid son of a bitch—you could've been killed!"

## Chapter Twenty-Four

Names: Dean Martin and Jerry Lewis

Year: 1949

Ages: 31 and 23

They hear the wild, ear-splitting screams erupt from just about everyone in the room except them before they see Frank Sinatra stepping into the light of the stage. As Jerry stares at that dark blue suit, those shoes that glint in the spotlight, the flower handkerchief in his breast pocket, all he can think about is how he wants to look cool like that. The screaming fans just about to die before a note even leaves his mouth, the

## The Crooner and The Comic

nice clothes that mean something—that mean you have money, security, success.

Jerry watches the performance on stage, sees the way Frank looks out at the audience as he sings, and sees himself doing it even better. He hears an uncertain note and shakes his head, smiling to himself. He could have sung that just right—he'd like to think as much, at least.

Dean stands there with his hands curled tightly around the railing, absorbing it all—the lights, the band, the music, the god-like character in the center of the stage, the fans. He feels this overwhelming weight on his shoulders, pressing him down and down, and he's not sure why. His hands grip the railing tighter as if that can make the frustration go away, but it doesn't.

\* \* \*

It's been over an hour, and the only words exchanged between Jerry and Dean since the concert was when Dean asked if he wanted to get coffee. So, here they are in a booth at the drugstore, Jerry sipping at his vanilla milkshake shamelessly, and Dean nursing a cup of black coffee.

Jerry's still energized from the whole experience, and wants to say something, but doesn't know what. He doesn't have to when Dean abruptly says with a strained voice, "Man, I couldn't believe the way that guy phrases a lyric."

"Yeah, it makes you feel—"

"Jealous! *That's* what it makes you feel!" For the first time that night, Dean lets himself look at what it is that makes his hands curl into fists at his sides and brows furrow. Jerry ponders being jealous of Frank's abilities, but after a moment

## Chapter Twenty-Four

shrugs.

"Yeah—I guess you're right. I kept seeing myself up there in front of four thousand screaming fans."

"It's great to live in a country where a kid from Hoboken, New Jersey, can have the world in the palm of his hand." Where a nobody can become a somebody, Dean doesn't say, but they both think it. They've been nobodies all their lives.

"Well, I guess we can dream." Jerry sighs wistfully, hand on his chin. He jumps when Dean suddenly slams his palm down on the table, making their glasses clink.

"Dreaming is for loafers who never do anything. I don't have time for dreams. I want action. I want a car and a home and all the things you get when you get there. If you don't push through the crowd, you'll be stuck here your whole life." Emerald eyes wide, Jerry just stares at Dean wordlessly. He has never heard Dean talk like this. He honestly thought that out of the two, he was the only one that had the big ambitions—that he was the dreamer.

"Well . . . " Jerry finally manages, not sure how to respond, "I bet my impression of Sinatra will be better tonight then it ever was before."

\* \* \*

*The Crooner and The Comic*

Names: Dean Martin and Jerry Lewis

Year: 1949

Ages: 31 and 23

As Dean steps up to his mark, waiting for the scene to begin, it strikes him as odd that Don didn't look very nervous at all. Given that Dean was about to punch him in the face, he was either very good at taking blows or very stupid. However, Dean didn't have time to voice his concerns when the yell echoed through the set, "And . . . ACTION!"

Dean gives himself the count of five seconds before opening the door in front of him leading to the set of Dianna's character's room and immediately wrapping his arms around her waist, exclaiming cheerily, "Jane, honey!"

"Uh, Steve! What are you doing here?" She stares at him with a petrified expression as Dean hugs her closer to himself.

"I'm so glad you sent for me!"

"That's cozy, but what about me!" Comes Don's voice from the opposite side of the room, and Dean steps away from Diana with raised brows.

"You?"

"Yes, me. I happen to have a date with Jane tonight." Don states matter-of-factly, clasping his hands together proudly.

"What goes on here?" Dean turns to Diana, hands on his

## Chapter Twenty-Four

hips.

"Yeah, what goes on here?" Don echoes. Diana smiles nervously, stammering, "Well, I—I don't know what to say!"

"Well, I know what to do!" With that, Dean turns on his heel and punches Don square in the jaw. Having done this enough times to know how to form a fist correctly, Dean knows his hand isn't broken, but he knows he's sure gonna feel it tomorrow. Diana cries out like she's supposed to, but Don doesn't get up and the director yells cut hurriedly.

"Hey, pallie, are you alright?" Dean kneels down beside Don and puts a hand on his shoulder, and a moment later Don turns his head so Dean can see the blood practically pouring from his mouth.

"You punched me!" Don manages as Diana pulls him up with a shocked expression.

"Yeah, I know! Oh . . . " Dean trails off when the pieces fit together in his mind. "Sorry, Don. I didn't know I wasn't supposed to. I'll pay for any work you gotta get done. Really, I'm sorry." As a few other staff members take Don away, Dean stares after them with a grimace. He really hadn't even thought about not actually punching Don, and nobody had told him otherwise!

He's jerked from his thoughts by someone laughing hysterically, and he glances around to find Jerry rolling on the ground, tears streaming down his cheeks.

"You . . . you . . . punched him!" Jerry manages through his peals of laughter, and Dean crosses his arms indignantly.

"How was I supposed to know?" Those words send Jerry into another fit, and Dean walks away shaking his head, a grin tugging at his lips. He actually punched him. You can take the boy out of Steubenville, but you can't take Steubenville out of the boy.

# Chapter Twenty-Five

~~~~~

Names: Dean Martin and Jerry Lewis

Year: 1949

Ages: 32 and 23

"Hey, Dean!" Jerry whispers excitedly, tugging at Dean's coat like a kid trying to get his dad's attention.
"What?" Dean says exasperatedly over the cigarette in his mouth.
"I think it's Perry Como!" He gestures over to someone strolling in their direction from the building marked 'Studio A', someone who walks an awful lot like Dean—so relaxed like that, with his hands in his pockets and probably a tune on his breath.
"Really?!" Dean straightens in his seat, trying to get a good

## The Crooner and The Comic

look at the guy's face—it *is* Perry! Dean isn't what he would call a fan of a lot of singers and actors; to be honest, he thought he could do what a lot of them did, but Perry Como is definitely one he respects. Although both Perry and Sinatra are Italian, and that gives them both a leg up in Dean's eyes, Sinatra acts like he's a god, but Dean knows what he does. He just sings, and to be honest Dean doesn't even understand why people pay him so much money to do something as simple as stand on stage and sing. He'd do it for free—he has.

"Let's say hi." Jerry urges Dean, but they don't have to as Perry recognizes them and makes a beeline to their table. Jerry watches in starstruck fascination, but Dean knows he's that way about almost every famous star they meet.

"Hi, I'm Perry. I've seen you two at the Copa before, and you're very funny." Both Dean and Jerry stand up instinctively, and shake his hand, surprised at how soft-spoken and . . . well, like he is on television. I mean, since when would someone like Perry Como introduce himself to them like they didn't know who he was?

Dean's impressed, but doesn't exactly make a show of it as he nonchalantly takes a drag from his cig and says, "Thanks, Perry. We appreciate that. We are real fans of yours, you know," Dean grins, sensing Perry's easygoing nature, and adds, "From one Bing to another." Perry laughs a soft, kind of sweet laugh, and says, "Aren't we all?"

Dean knows Jerry well enough to know he'd do well to get a word in before Jerry started up his Idiot schtick that he always fell into when he was nervous or just trying to impress someone. So, he's glad he did when Jerry taps Perry on the shoulder and then clasps his hands together, gasping dramatically in his exaggerated deep voice, "It's really you, Mr.

## Chapter Twenty-Five

Como! It's really you! Right next to me! Oh, I might die!" He always has to be schmaltzy.

Perry chuckles in amusement and runs a hand over his face before checking his watch and saying earnestly, "Look, boys, I'd love to stay and chat, really I would, but I've got an appointment I gotta keep. Listen, you guys keep up the great work, and I'll definitely try to stop by another one of your shows. Maybe some of your craziness'll rub off on me." With that, Perry smiles to himself and continues on his way, whistling "Oh, Marie."

Dean watches him walk away, and thinks to himself. Maybe he'll invite Perry to go golfing with him sometime.

\* \* \*

Names: Dean Martin and Jerry Lewis

Year: 1949

Ages: 32 and 23

Step, step, step. Puff. Step, step, step. Puff. Jerry is starting to feel dizzy just watching Dean pacing and smoking from end to end of the room like a man about to meet a grim fate. He's in his newly pressed tuxedo, and his hand keeps reaching up to his bow tie as if to loosen it, but then it falters and drops to his side again, where it curls and uncurls in a fist. Jerry's heart is racing like crazy, and he's starting to feel like *he's* the one getting married the more he watches Dean.

"Christ, I need a drink!" Dean finally blurts out, turning to Jerry with wide eyes. Jerry smiles in relief, and takes the opportunity.

"You're gonna be alright if I leave for a minute, right?"

"Of course!" Dean shouts, gesturing for Jerry to leave. "Get the drink!" Practically sprinting through the house to get to the pantry, Jerry is glad for the distraction. The moment he opens the door to the pantry, an involuntary gasp escapes his lips. There are shelves upon shelves stacked to the ceiling of enough drinks to get all of Pasadena loaded.

He scans the nearest section of bottles until he finds the Johnnie Walker Black Label, and then looks for a tumbler. Oh man. Jerry catches sight of a massive tumbler that's gotta hold at least sixteen ounces, and grins. There's never a bad time for a gag. He fills it to the brim and strolls nonchalantly back to Dean's room.

It takes a second for Dean to register the tumbler because his mind is going in a thousand directions at once, but once he does, he doubles over in uncharacteristically hysterical laughter that leaves him gasping for breath. Jerry shakes his head and places the cup on the bedside table. He knows that Dean's just nervous out of his nitwit, and needs to get all of that out of him. When he's halfway composed himself, Dean takes a few swallows of the stuff and lights another cigarette.

Jerry watches Dean for a minute, torn, as he tries to decide how he wants to say what he's thinking. Finally he begins, "Can I ask you a personal question?" If it weren't for the gravity of the situation, Jerry would have burst out laughing right then and there—he knows Dean too well to ask anymore, though it's not like he ever did. Dean stares at him inquisitively, letting his cigarette hang from between his lips. Jerry can hardly meet

## Chapter Twenty-Five

his eyes, but just lets it all out anyhow. "You just got out of one marriage . . . what the hell are you rushing into another one for?"

Dean doesn't move; doesn't say a word. Jerry suddenly feels like he was punched in the gut, and hurriedly adds, "Forgive me, Paul. Jeanne's a great girl, and I think she would follow you to the ends of the earth. I know she would wait until you were ready. And there are four kids to think about." It's mostly true on Jerry's part. He won't admit he's jealous of Jeanne. To be fair, it's not like Dean doesn't know.

The cigarette trembles slightly within Dean's grasp as he brings it to his lips, gaze focused on some point on the wall behind Jerry. Finally he says with a serious voice, "Listen, Jer. You know me better than anyone, so what I say is between us . . ." Despite it all, Jerry feels a little thrill of pride at that. "I do worry about my kids. But this feels so *right*. So *strong*."

At those words, something finally occurs to Jerry about Dean. He must really love Jeanne . . . and it seems as if this may be the first time. Betty's a great girl, and she and Dean had some great, wonderful times together, but it just wasn't right for Dean . . . it wasn't love.

He nods, and sees the relief flood Dean's face.

"It's your life, pal. And you have to do what's best for you. You've always taken care of your kids; now it's your turn to take care of yourself. Everything'll fall into place." The most genuine smile Jerry's seen from him all week breaks onto his face, and Dean wraps his arms around him in a bear hug, whispering, "Thanks, Jer."

# Chapter Twenty-Six

Names: Dean Martin and Jerry Lewis

Year: 1949

Ages: 32 and 23

"Gee, that looks awful, Jer! Did *I* do that to you?!" Dean comes up from behind Jerry, who is just changing his shirt to get ready for them going out to dinner, and gapes at the massive bruise down the one side of Jerry's back and ribs.

Jerry jerks away from Dean and sheepishly pulls his shirt on. "Oh that? It's nothing, really! I'm just a little sore, that's all."

"*Just a little sore?!* Jer, your back's practically purple! Was that from when I pushed you on the ground?" Jerry can't see his face, but from the strain in Dean's voice, he can just imagine those eyes filled with worry and lips pressed together.

## Chapter Twenty-Six

"Maybe, I'm not sure-but really, Dean, let's just go! It doesn't hurt, honest!" Jerry exclaims, but it's only half-hearted, because if he's being truthful with himself, his back is killing him.

"Oh, really? So if I do this . . . " Pain shoots through Jerry's back and he has to bite down on his lip to keep from crying out. He spins around to face Dean with watery eyes.

"What the hell, Dean?! A bruise is a bruise! If you punch it, it's gonna hurt!"

"I barely touched you, Germ." Dean's grin is short lived, though, as worry once again crosses his face while watching Jerry struggle to shrug on his shirt.

"You should really tell me if I hurt you. I told you this was going to happen sometime if you make me horse around with you!" Dean's voice suddenly rises in anger, and he glares at a shocked Jerry.

"This isn't your fault, and it *certainly* isn't mine! It was an accident, so what are you yelling at me for?" Dean sighs and takes out a cigarette. Jerry's right, of course, but Dean just can't bear the thought of *him* hurting Jerry.

"Sorry for yellin', kid. I'm not mad at you." He says softly. He's just mad at himself. All things considered, Dean's a little surprised at himself. This isn't the first time either one of them have woken up and discovered bruises they don't remember getting. But Dean also knows he's the kind of guy who only needs one moment for anger to take him over, or for him to just get caught up in the excitement of it all. But he's seen the way the Kid looks at him after he gets in a fight with some fat-head: a little admiration, a little fear. He would never let himself hurt the kid. Never.

\* \* \*

## The Crooner and The Comic

Names: Dean Martin and Jerry Lewis

Year: 1949

Ages: 32 and 23

If someone was gonna plug you, would they call you to their office? Eh, they'd probably do it while you're asleep. Jerry shrugs to himself and straightens his suit, trying to stop the corner of his mouth from twitching nervously.

Finally he plucks up the courage to swing the door of the office open and walk right up to Moe, who's sitting at his desk smoking a cigar.

"Siddown." Moe motions towards the chair at the opposite side of the desk, beady eyes narrowed. Not a good sign. "You realize you owe this hotel $137,000." Moe states, half-asking, half-telling Jerry.

"And you realize that you're running this hotel, and you're giving that kind of credit to someone that's getting $7,500 a week. Doesn't that make you an idiot?" Jerry can't help himself, and for a frightening moment as Moe just stares at him with smoke slowly coming from the corner of his mouth, he thinks this is it. But finally Moe says, "Well, yeah. I guess so."

"You guess so? I'm just a kid, and you let me run up a $137,000 marker? Where in the hell do you think I'm gonna get that kind of money from?" Damn it! Once he starts, he just can't stop himself.

"Well, that's just it. How *do* you propose to pay it?" The very first thought that pops into Jerry's mind of running away is a ludicrous one, and he ignores it as soon as it appears. That

## Chapter Twenty-Six

would be a good way to get himself killed. His second idea has to do with Fischetti and those other guys back in New York, who would probably give him way more leeway.

"Call New York and ask how I should pay it. I'll follow those instructions."

"Alright, then, Kid. I'll find you when they tell me what they want you to do." With that, Jerry is ushered out of Moe's office, both relieved and panicked at the same time. Well, there goes all that money he was thrilled about making.

# Chapter Twenty-Seven

Names: Dean Martin and Jerry Lewis

Year: 1949

Ages: 33 and 24

"Hi, sweetheart." Jerry stands from the couch to give Patti a quick kiss, but he senses something is wrong as she pulls herself gently away from him to sit a few spaces away. "What is it? Who was on the phone?"

Patti just stares down at her lap, smoothing out her skirt with steady hands. The serene, yet somehow intangibly discontent, expression that's settled on her face strikes Jerry once again by how beautiful she is. She bites her lower lip, trying to decide

## Chapter Twenty-Seven

what to say—or what not to say—before finally answering softly, "I was just talking to Betty."

"Oh." Is all Jerry can say as his heart drops. He has an idea what's bothering Patti, and it's not one he's exactly thrilled to discuss. "What did she say?"

"She told me about the divorce. I don't like this, Jerry. I don't like this at all." Patti finally looks up at Jerry with hardened eyes, and she continues, "Betty's a great girl, and she's gone through a lot taking care of Dean's kids, what with him being away nearly all the time. And now . . . " Her voice abruptly breaks, and she takes a second to compose herself. "Now he does *this* to her."

Jerry feels a surge of anger, and his voice rises as he tries to defend Dean like he's defending his own reputation, "That's completely unfair! You're only looking at one side of things, Patti! Dean *has* to work away from home to support them, and he's always been there for them when they need him! Besides, it's not like Betty's totally innocent. She's been drinking, and it's starting to affect his kids. Bottomline, if Dean wants out because he's not happy, he's entitled to it!" He feels somewhat lightheaded when he finishes, and is a little surprised by how strongly he is on Dean's side.

Patti is shaking her head, cheeks flushed. Her lips are pressed together into two thin white lines, and she seems as if she's stopping herself from saying something. Jerry thinks for a moment he's won until Patti says in a soft, strained voice, "I'm sorry, but I just don't agree. This is unfair to Betty, and I feel like you're not looking at the situation without bias because of Dean. I'm sorry, Jer, but I just don't think I can be friends with Dean anymore if he's going to go through with this."

That is of course, the wrong thing to say, for Jerry's eyes

## The Crooner and The Comic

narrow, and he shoots back with intended spite, "If you turn your back on him, you're gonna hurt me, because Dean's my friend. Do you understand what that means?" Of course Patti understands what he means, and for a moment Jerry feels a stab of guilt at the hurt that flashes across Patti's face. How could she forget last year's . . . separation?

As expected, Patti looks down and whispers, "I'll do my best, if that's what you want."

\* \* \*

Names: Dean Martin and Jerry Lewis

Year: 1949

Ages: 33 and 24

"Hey, Paul? I was just thinkin'." Jerry's voice is unusually hesitant, so Dean glances up from his comic book curiously. Curled up on the couch like a little kid, hugging his knees to his chest, Jerry glances up at Dean and then back down to see his reaction before continuing.

"That's dangerous." The Kid snickers at that, but then his face hardens, trying to keep serious for whatever he's trying to say. An unusual sight indeed. "Well, go on!"

"Okay . . . well, we've been partners for about three years, you know?" Jerry peeks up furtively at Dean, being very cautious about the whole thing, and at this point Dean's starting to feel uneasy.

## Chapter Twenty-Seven

"Come on, just let it out already!"

"I've watched you for a while, trying to understand the way you . . . well, the way you are. But I don't think I understand still. You act like you don't give a damn about anyone other than yourself, and it's like you don't feel—or at the very least you don't let anyone know that you do." Dean puts down the book and crosses his arms with a slightly wide-eyed stare. His expression is not exactly one of being offended, more of surprised contemplation, so Jerry's encouraged to continue. "I mean, Paul, I just don't get it. I know that's not really you, and I don't understand why you don't—why you *refuse* to let anyone in. Is it a tryna be cool thing? What—just what is it?" It's almost like Jerry's words hang in the air for moments after, and Dean gazes at Jerry unblinkingly, cheeks flushed beneath that dark tan skin. He wordlessly crawls off the bed and sits down beside Jerry on the couch, his instinctively relaxed form the complete opposite of Jerry's.

"Where do ya get that idea from, Kid? You know about me, I know just everything about you."

"Such a headache you give me. Come on, don't mess with me, Dean. You know perfectly well what I'm talking about. It's just that I . . . well, I want to know why." Jerry stops kind of breathlessly, staring up at Dean with an earnest glint in his eyes—like he means what he said, but is still hoping that he doesn't make him mad.

Normally such a question would be followed by Dean standing up and leaving the room, or a punch in the arm. But Jerry's different. There's something so unassuming, so . . . non-threatening about the Kid that Dean somehow always finds his defenses faltering.

"Well, you know how I grew up, Jer. This is just how I gotta

*The Crooner and The Comic*

be. I'm no sissy, and so just cus' I don't flip my lid all the time don't mean anything." The answer is far from what Jerry is looking for, but as he studies Dean beside him, who is barely able to meet his eyes, he knows that's as much as he can ask for. Saying *that* much is putting a noticeable strain on Dean, whose brows seem to be permanently knitted together.

The pieces of the puzzle have been coming into place slowly, very slowly for Jerry, but the picture is becoming clearer. He's met Dean parents, and been around Italian families like theirs; Dean likely grew up being told feelings are for fags or broads. It makes you weak, and it'll only end up breaking your heart. But Jerry's not stupid, and he's *certainly* not oblivious. He knows that even if Dean doesn't want to face them, there are still very real, very strong feelings swirling around inside him.

There are times when it's early in the morning, and Dean is in a particularly philosophical mood, or they're sitting silently together staring out at the sun just peeking over the horizon, that Jerry's sure for a moment he just caught a glimpse of the real Dean. The Dean who truly cares for him, and who's a little scared about how he feels about the world around him.

If it's this hard for him to understand Dean, with a pang of guilt Jerry wonders how much harder it must be for Jeanne. He's seen them together, and heard from Patti; it's no secret that they hardly talk anymore. Maybe that's why Jeanne always seems uptight around him. She's jealous.

## Chapter Twenty-Eight

Names: Dean Martin and Jerry Lewis

Year: 1950

Ages: 33 and 24

To have your hometown name a *day* after you, throw a whole parade in your honor, and to be able to return to those old friends and enemies triumphant and with all the world on your side would thrill anyone. Anyone, that is, except Dean Martin.

Dean wishes he were anywhere but in Steubenville. Even the name makes him sick to his stomach. As always, though, such a response doesn't lead Dean to wonder why he feels this way. And he doesn't need to because Jerry does enough wondering for the both of them.

The day goes by in a blur for Jerry, and he can hardly keep track of rugged face after rugged face of Dean's old friends that never really seemed to exist in real life until now. Although he expected to feel out of place because Steubenville isn't his home town, Jerry is pleasantly surprised by the pride that runs through him of being associated with Dean as they meet old pals of his and perform at just about every place capable of holding a couple hundred people.

Despite how thrilled he is, Jerry can't help noticing something's off about Dean. He knows Dean better than anyone else, but even he is puzzled at first by Dean's seeming hatred of this warm hometown reception. Jerry knows that if he was in Dean's shoes, he would have a ball going back to Newark in all of his glory and throwing it in the faces of those who thought he would never succeed.

But then again, Dean and Jerry are very different people. By the end of the day, Jerry feels he understands why Dean is unsettled. This whole day must have been a big, glaring sign to Dean of where he came from, and who he really was: a small, dirty nobody from a small, dirty town of steel mills and gangsters. Jerry can even understand why Dean left Betty. She was just another reminder.

As intelligent as Jerry is, he doesn't know the half of the well of hatred and scorn that lies deep, deep within Dean.

Sitting at the bar surrounded by old friends, all Dean can think about is that the lives all of them—Mindy, Ross, Jiggs, Smuggs, all of them—are spent in every waking moment searching for, clawing at, what Dean has. He's got the wife. He's got kids. He's got world fame and more money and girls than any of them would know what to do with. And that's all

## Chapter Twenty-Eight

there is? That's the end of things? If that's so, then death isn't imminent; it's here already.

\* \* \*

Names: Dean Martin & Jerry Lewis

Year: 1950

Ages: 33 and 24

"Jerry? Jer? Where are you? Everyone's looking for ya!" Dean calls out, though only loud enough for Jerry to hear were he close by, being too tired to try any harder. He's about to scratch his head and turn right back around to his dressing room when he catches sight of the skinny, crouched figure on the catwalk belonging to his partner—what's that Kid doing this time?

He makes out enough words between Jerry and a somewhat annoyed-looking sound technician to guess Jerry's on a discovery crusade again. Asking how everything works around the set, and then some.

"Are the catwalks made of two-by-fours?"

"Are they built on a temporary basis?"

"How do they hang them?"

The Kid's even been buying his own cameras like food, and making these home parodies of popular movies—it's great that he's interested in these sorts of things; who is Dean to tell him what to like?

But at the same time, it always makes Dean feel a little mad.

## The Crooner and The Comic

Jerry's always trying to learn more, sure, but it always seems sort of . . . forced. Like he's trying to do it just to show people he can. That the funny-looking Jew isn't a monkey; he's smart and knows everything about moviemaking.

## Chapter Twenty-Nine

Names: Dean Martin and Jerry Lewis

Year: 1950

Ages: 33 and 24

Dean lets himself loosen up as he hops up the stairs of the stage leading up to the makeshift throne, sitting slouched with arms and legs nonchalantly hanging over the sides. Finally he says, making no effort to conceal his less than educated accent, "Pops, look at me! I'm sittin' on de throne!"

The actor who plays his dad in the scene bursts out laughing, having only seen the more composed side of Dean, and so do some of the behind the scenes crew. Dean himself even cracks a grin. But one person in that rehearsal does not find it so

## The Crooner and The Comic

funny. Well, he does think Dean's funny, but he just wishes the laughs were directed at him.

Gritting his teeth, as much as Jerry hates the person inside of him who's desperate, so desperate he'd do anything to take the attention away from Dean, or if he can't, make all the rest of them suffer for it, he gives in.

"Ahh!" Jerry groans, clutching at his head and making it seem as if he can barely stand. His little charade quickly does its job, for many of the crew rush up to him and help him sit down, trying to figure out what's wrong with him. A migraine, the doctor there says to everyone, and the whole affair makes Jerry feel better, but barely.

Why? Because the entire time everyone swarms around Jerry, Dean stands back from the crowd, head tilted slightly as he stares at him with the strangest expression on his face. In the one moment their eyes meet, Jerry knows what that expression means and wishes he didn't.

Dean knows what he's doing. He knows and he hates Jerry for it. But not as much as Jerry hates himself for it.

\* \* \*

## Chapter Twenty-Nine

Names: Dean Martin and Jerry Lewis

Year: 1951

Ages: 34 and 25

"I'm getting out of this, it's like wearing a board." Jerry mutters as he unbuckles his seatbelt and begins to unbutton the jacket of his tux. Dean nods eagerly in agreement before doing the same. They've got enough of a car ride to the Hudson that they have no hesitation before taking off their jackets and pants, but when they catch sight of the driver in the rearview mirror peeking at them with a quizzical, somewhat concerned, expression.

   Dean and Jerry look at each other and begin to giggle at the hilarity of the situation, or because they're so exhausted they can no longer control themselves, and those giggles turn into breath-catching laughter.

\* \* \*

Thirty minutes later Dean and Jerry find themselves in a sticky situation, and the driver quickly pulls out of the jammed line of cars to the side of the road. Having expected to have to just hide behind a bush somewhere or *something*, they are relieved when they spot a convenience store.

   Jumping out of the car, Jerry and Dean enter the store. Jerry in leather boots, shorts, and a shirt. Dean in patent-leather loafers, shorts, and a shirt. Jerry feels a little self-conscious as other customers in the store stop with strange looks on their face, but is able to play it off as a joke given everyone in the store obviously knows who they are. Dean couldn't give a crap.

There are about seven other people there in all, and they all want autographs. That's fine, despite the hurry and the situation. When someone steps up asking for a photograph, Dean and Jerry look at each other and promptly say together, "No, thank you."

When they've finished up in the store, they head back to the limo, only to be stopped by two highway patrol officers who are not only big enough to easily take them out, but mad enough to. Despite the quickening of his heart and the nervousness that floods through him almost instinctively, Dean just says with a completely straight face, "Please, Officer, give us a break. I'm his lawyer and he's on parole. This could go very badly for him."

It's exactly what they need to catch a break, and the officers laugh, all troubles forgotten as they shake hands with Dean and Jerry and ask for autographs.

## Chapter Thirty

Names: Dean Martin and Jerry Lewis

Year: 1951

Ages: 34 and 25

Dean wraps his trench coat tighter around himself, disappointed that even inside the cab he can't escape the oddly wintry air this morning. Jerry must notice it's cold, too, because with a huff he looks away from the window and says, more to himself than anything, "It's July. What the hell's winter still doing here?"

Dean's about to chuckle—bitterly, at that—when he spots the crowd spilling into the street. He hopes for a second that maybe they're not waiting for them, but of course he's wrong as he sees they're at the Paramount Theater, and his heart sinks as he realizes there's no clean way out of this. They've got to go through the crowds to get to the backstage door.

As their cab begins to nose its way through the crowd to get to the curb, no directions have to be given as Dean and Jerry slouch in their seats, either pulling down a hat or raising the collar of a coat to conceal their identity. It's no use, though, for even before they reach the curb, they begin to hear muffled shouts outside and see people pointing.

"It's them!"

"We'd better hurry the hell up when we reach the curb." Jerry says anxiously to Dean, face still turned away from any of the windows as if eye contact with one of the fans would be just as bad as being out there.

Finally it's time, and Dean and Jerry share a pale glance before making the mad scramble out of the cab. The curb's on the right side of the cab, and so Jerry gets to make the dash first. When Dean finally emerges from the car, there's so many fans around him, pressing on each side. The biting chill of the air abruptly feels heavier and warmer, and the thought passes through Dean's mind that if he tripped or fell, he wouldn't be able to get up again . . . fear courses through his veins, sending him surging forward, but something jerks him back.

Shooting a desperate look behind him, he realizes the people around him shut the door on the tail of his trench coat. Tugging on it as if his life depends on it—which he thinks it does—he hears Jerry shout over the fray, "Leave the coat, for goodness' sake!" One more tug and he realizes Jerry's right. Damn it, that was his favorite coat.

Shrugging it off into the hands of a happy fan, Dean bolts through the crowd closely after Jerry, a primal desire to live fueling him.

## Chapter Thirty

They don't stop until they're in the elevator, and for once Dean doesn't mind it, for even this seems exponentially more bearable than the chaos back there. The elevator doors slide closed, shutting out the frenzied cries from outside, and an abrupt, uneasy silence descends upon them except for their short, ragged breaths.

Not a word is ever spoken about that between them.

\* \* \*

Names: Dean Martin and Jerry Lewis

Year: 1951

Ages: 34 and 25

"No, no, I'll come with." Dean says shortly, stepping up onto the first ledge of the ambulance, grabbing a hold of one of the doors to fully hoist himself inside, but Dick grabs him by the sleeve. Dick's eyes are narrowed, and with a meaty hand bigger even than Dean's, he keeps grasp of him.

"Are you sure, Dean? We don't need Martin *and* Lewis in the hospital." A hint of brevity for the sake of keeping calm, but the concern is apparent. The thought of the cramped, hectic space in the back of the ambulance makes Dean's teeth clench, but he nods nevertheless. He's got to be there for Jerry.

Dick nods grimly, and pats him comfortingly on the back. "You're doin' the right thing, Dino."

## The Crooner and The Comic

    Dean then turns to the ambulance and climbs inside to the back between EMTs and others unknown to him. Finally he forces himself to look at Jerry lying on the stretcher.

    Strapped down and stripped of his jacket and bowtie, with shirt unbuttoned just enough so Dean can see the rapid rise and fall of his skinny chest, Jerry doesn't really seem to notice Dean's there. His face is ashen, and every few moments he'll shut his eyes with an expression twisted in pain.

    Dean's stomach churns as the fall passes through his mind . . . the terrible moment he and Jerry locked eyes in the air, *knowing* it was going to happen . . . then the sickening thud and the collective, sudden gasp of horror from the audience.

    Abruptly aware the ambulance is moving as a little bump on the road jolts him from his thoughts, it takes him a second to wonder if the drive'll hurt Jerry more. He hates that he's right when the ambulance jolts once more, and a low groan kind of falteringly leaves Jerry's lips.

    Dean grimaces, heart racing in his chest . . . he doesn't want to see this. "Hey, doc!" Turning to one of the EMTs, Dean asks in an unusually desperate tone, "Can'cha give the kid something for the pain?" The EMTs a young guy, not much older than Dean, and he seems torn, glancing from Dean to Jerry, and then finally nodding.

    After a few minutes Jerry relaxes and looks to Dean through heavy-lidded eyes glazed over from the drugs. Dean squeezes his hand reassuringly, and the edges of Jerry's lips curve upwards.

* * *

    Finally the ambulances comes to a stop, and to Dean's dismay

## Chapter Thirty

they end up filing into this elevator the size of a shoe box. Dean only has room to turn his head; Jerry and two other medical assistants take up all the room, and Dean's starting to struggle a little for breath.

Loosening his tie, Dean can't help envisioning the mad push to leave the elevator if need be—how he just wouldn't be able to leave . . . could he pull the doors open if he had to? And if he could, would he just see wall? Concrete that can't be torn through?

Dean gasps out, sweat popping out from his temple. When his wild eyes meet Jerry's, the Kid somehow reads his expression even in the midst of the haze of drugs and pain—he always does— and speaks for the first time since the fall: "You'll do anything, won't you, fellow?"

Dean takes a deep breath and offers him a smile. Apparently so, Kid . . . apparently so.

# Chapter Thirty-One

Names: Dean Martin and Jerry Lewis

Year: 1951

Ages: 34 and 25

"Hey, Paul! I finally got them to make those changes they've been needing to make on my character!" Jerry's voice is ecstatic on the other end of the phone, and Dean chuckles.

"Good for you, Kid." He doesn't need to ask what changes were made; he knows Jerry would tell him even if Dean asked him *not* to.

"I just *knew* the guy I'm playing was too . . . one-sided, ya know? He's all moron and no heart. I got them to accept the backstory for him so that the audience can really identify with him. You know, the way you do when you watch Chaplain in

## Chapter Thirty-One

"The Circus", and how much . . . how much *pathos* there was? That's what I want to be like . . . " Jerry's voice trails off.

"That's great, Jer—" Dean drawls, only to be interrupted by a beep on the phone signalling there's someone else on the line calling him. "Sorry, I gotta go, someone else is calling me."

"Alright, thanks anyway." Jerry sounds somewhat distracted, but that could just be the reception. Dean shakes his head and goes onto the other line. Normally he wouldn't bother, but this conversation was making Dean a little squeamish.

"Hey, Dino! Did I catch you at a bad time?" Dean recognizes it immediately as Bill from the golf course, and takes a casual drag. He's a nice guy, if anything just a smite too talkative.

"No, not at all, Bill."

"Good! I just wanted to say, I saw your show last night, and gee whiz you're really a smash!"

"Thanks, Bill. We try." The Kid always tells him he doesn't try hard enough.

"No, really, Dino! I mean, Jerry's great and all, but you've obviously got something yourself! I mean, you're funny—really funny—and you're better than Como." Tell the papers that.

"Thanks, Bill. That's nice. Listen, I'll see you on Saturday, but I've gotta run." Dean says tersely, almost surprised at the frustration that boils up within him.

"Alright, Dino, see you around." Clicking the phone back onto its base, Dean exhales loudly and folds his arms across his chest. Maybe he could make it by himself. Hell, who even knows anymore. Jerry sure *seems* to be doing better, anyhow. He's trying to become like Charlie Chaplain. Well, Chaplain didn't need some Italian crooner.

\* \* \*

*The Crooner and The Comic*

Names: Dean Martin and Jerry Lewis

Year: 1951

Ages: 34 and 25

Laughter. High-pitched, tittering giggles Jerry instantly recognizes as Gary's, followed by soft, but amused laughter from Patti. Rubbing the sleep from his eyes, Jerry stretches his stiff limbs and leaps nimbly from the couch to peek into the kitchen where the noise is emanating from. In an almost picture-perfect scene, Jerry sees Patti guiding Gary's hands to knead the dough, and Ronnie sitting safely on the counter opposite them with a frown set in his chubby face that's hard for Jerry not to grin at. They're making cookies.

The sweet, familiar scent of freshly made dough wafts toward him so his stomach growls. He didn't eat all day at work, and as soon as he got home he was too tired to do anything other than sleep.

When Gary jumps off the stool, scampering across the kitchen to grab the cookie cutters, Jerry sees his curly, brown hair that is now about the color of Ronnie's blond locks from the flour that's also smeared across his face.

Once he brings the cutters over and climbs back onto the stool to lay them on the counter, Pattie turns to Ronnie with a smile. His eyes light up as he realizes it's his turn, and he holds out his arms expectantly for her to lift him onto the other counter.

As Jerry watches silently from the doorway, the bright lights from the kitchen not quite reaching him, his smile fades.

## Chapter Thirty-One

When's the last time Gary and Ronnie smiled like that around him? When's the last time he made them that happy? A lump forms in his throat as he realizes what he's done. He remembers the nights spent curled up in bed or behind a couch, crying warm, useless tears because his mom and dad weren't there . . . If it weren't for Patti, he would've been the cause of his own kid's tears. He would have made his own kids feel the same way he did. Unwanted. Useless. A nobody.

*I'll come home early from now on*, Jerry vows to himself. *I'll make more time to play baseball, or go fishing, or watch movies with them. I'll try harder.*

# Chapter Thirty-Two

Names: Dean Martin and Jerry Lewis

Year: 1951

Ages: 34 and 25

"Please listen to me, oh Marie, 'we Marie!" Dean finishes his song quickly, with an almost unnoticeable shake of his head and self-deprecating smirk, and they march off the stage together, heading straight into the dressing room amidst anonymous pats on the back and 'Good show's.

Jerry wasn't going to say anything, he really didn't have any plans to mention it, but as Dean strips off his jacket and bowtie, cigarette already between his lips, Jerry bursts out, "Just once, would you sing a song straight?"

Dean's fingers falter on the bowtie for a moment, and he

## Chapter Thirty-Two

shoots Jerry an odd expression. "I do."

"No, you don't."

"I think I'd know if I didn't sing a song straight." Jerry doesn't get what Dean's kidding himself for. Well, Dean's obviously not gonna admit it, so Jerry knows he's going to have to come up with another solution.

"You know something? You're doing so good in your spot, maybe I'm coming on too early." Is Dean going to buy it? Nope.

"Screw you! Whattaya talkin' about? You're gonna spoil what we got. Forget it."

**Two Weeks Later**

Jerry's eyes narrow as they come to the end of the article he's reading. He glances back through it just to make sure he didn't miss something, but he comes back to the end with the same conclusion. *The Chronicle* had written a whole page about Martin and Lewis without mentioning Martin once!

He peeks out of the corner of his eyes to see if Dean notices the same thing, and his heart drops. Other than the newspaper clutched tightly in Dean's hands, there's no other indication of something being off except for the look in his eyes. It's like they've visibly darkened, and his eyebrows are knitted together slightly.

Clearing his throat, Jerry begins to say whatever he can to combat the article—for himself as much as for Dean. "You know something? They're always going to like the kid who makes the biggest noise." Although that's true, Jerry can't help the thrill of pride he felt reading the article—they always make him seem like some sort of comic genius. "They're always going to pay attention to the monkey. You're going to hear

## The Crooner and The Comic

more about him than the straight man." That's because the monkey's funnier. "Nobody ever talked about George Burns. It was always Gracie. When Jack Benny and Mary Livingston worked in vaudeville, they didn't know who Jack Benny was."

Dean doesn't meet Jerry's pleading eyes, so Jerry continues, "You have to know that the straight man is never given the kudos that the comic gets. And I just need to know that you're okay with that."

A muscle jumps in Dean's jaw, and he finally turns to Jerry, saying, "Jerry, look. Your father told you once, be a hit. With the monkey act, with a couple of broads, with two balls and a watermelon. Whatever—just be a hit. We're a big hit. And you need to know that I know when our film is on that screen and *I* start to sing, the kids go for the popcorn."

"I don't think that's true." Jerry retorts, but he knows Dean's right—they come to watch the comic, not the crooner. But he feels like he has to keep arguing for Dean's sake—the look on his face makes Jerry's chest tighten. "I don't think little kids go for popcorn at any particular time."

Dean grabs his coat and jams a cigarette in his mouth. "Look, Jer, I've just gotta get some air, okay?" He's not really asking, though, and stalks out of the dressing room. Heart racing, Jerry watches the door close behind him and falls back into a chair, defeated.

\* \* \*

## Chapter Thirty-Two

Names: Dean Martin and Jerry Lewis

Year: 1952

Ages: 34 and 25

"Hey, shut up, you bozo. It's not like you know any better than the rest of us." Ray's about to respond when he takes an exaggerated sniff of the air in the limo. Jerry frowns, having just been hit with an odd smell. It's not exactly . . . rancid, but it sure isn't apple pie. He glances to Dean in confusion, who's wearing an amused smile. Ray from beside Dean yells up to Dick, "Gimme a hit!"

It finally dawns on Jerry what the smell is, and he watches curiously as the joint is passed around the limo—to everyone except him. He can barely see them, though, as it's the dead of night, and the snow whirling around outside with a temper blocks any moonlight from entering the limo.

"Hey! What is this shit? I'm twenty-five, for heaven's sake! Give me that thing!" Jerry calls up to Dick, who is now holding the joint, and can see clearly enough to catch the knowing expression that is exchanged between Dick and Dean.

"Okay, kid, go slow."

As soon as Jerry gets it, he does the exact opposite, inhaling as deeply as he had seen the others do. Big mistake. Dean's spot on when he yells gleefully, "Let the coughing begin!" Jerry can't catch a breath for five straight minutes as coughs rack his body mercilessly.

And, whether out of curiosity, or just plain stupidity, Jerry calls out hoarsely, "Hey, lemme try again!"

## The Crooner and The Comic

"Here's a new one guys." Dick shakes his head in bemusement, and Dean obediently hands it to Jerry again. This time Jerry takes it slow.

Not half an hour passes before the car is silent, with everyone being in a world of their own. Jerry's mind is drifting—he wonders for a moment if his body is, too— then he spends he doesn't know how long staring at a snowflake on the outside of the window for no apparent reason.

\* \* \*

Finally they're at West Lafayette. After eleven damn hours. Dean swears to himself he won't let Jerry talk him into something like this again. He's still feeling a little groggy from the drive and the joint, but as soon as the limo door is flung open, and he climbs out into the night—well, early morning—the fierce, snowy wind that buffers against him and stings his eyes sure changes that. Every breath takes in a lungful of air colder than the next, but he just focuses on the glaring light from the hotel getting nearer and nearer with every labored step.

Five minutes and a hilariously unrepeatable joke later, Dean, Jerry, and about four security men are on the way up to their suite. Jerry's still laughing so hard that his bloodshot eyes are brimming with tears, and he can barely walk through the hallway—though that may be the joint.

The joke wasn't *that* funny, and Dean frowns to himself as Jerry leans heavily on him and one of the security men. He shouldn't have let him smoke it, he's never done something like that before, and he's just a kid besides. A kid? He would have laughed at himself if he wasn't so worried—it seems like

## Chapter Thirty-Two

a day ago Jerry was a scrawny, gangly kid of nineteen who looked all of fifteen. Now . . . Jerry's filled out some, not a lot, and he's twenty freaking five years old. When did that happen?

"Hey, Jew. Listen to me." Dean begins quietly when Jerry's giggles seem to have subsided for the better, and proceeds to explain all the basics of a new pot smoker being vulnerable and what have you, but it doesn't do much good. Before he knows it, Jerry is singing—more like yelling—at the top of his lungs, and the security men look to Dean desperately as they know he's probably waking up the entire hotel.

Dean does just about everything he can but cover Jerry's mouth, and it does nothing. Geez, he should have known this would happen to Jerry. He has the liquor tolerance of a five-year-old, why would this be any different?

\* \* \*

Another ten minutes pass, and the security guards have left after getting Jerry into bed, still singing at that—could they tie him to the bedposts, Dean had wondered. A knock on the door brings a very concerned house detective in who looks as tired as Dean feels.

"What's going on up here, sir? We've got at least a dozen complaints—" He stops when he sees Jerry in bed, who cracks open his eyes, and upon seeing the detective, throws back the covers with a renewed burst of energy. Leaping out of bed, Jerry says, all too loudly and intermixed with random giggles, "I smoked pot. It was good. It can last for days with someone new. Like me! I'm new. I'll be better in a couple days—"

He's cut off by Dean wrapping a big hand around his upper

arm and steering him back to the bed, saying—more for the house detective's sake, than anything—"Come on, Jer, why don't you go back and get some rest." While he's struggling to get Jerry back under the covers, he casts a pleading glance to the house detective, who clears his throat and says, "I'll, uh, let you take care of this."

Once he's left the suite, Dean refocuses his attention on Jerry, who, like a child, is with shut eyes trying to take off his dress pants without actually getting up from the bed. Dean waits, patiently getting jostled, until Jerry has somehow managed to slip off his pants over his shoes—after all, he's the one who let Jerry take a smoke of the blasted thing.

He hopes Jerry's also going to take off his jacket and shoes, but just as soon as Jerry's done with his pants, he drops back onto the pillow like a rock. Fast asleep.

With a heavy sigh that's more concerned than frustrated, Dean slips Jerry's limp, bony arms from the jacket sleeves and lifts him easily from the bed just enough to get the jacket entirely from under him. This Kid. When he's asleep is the only time all the anxieties, all the fears, all the sorrows leave him. The furrow between his brows is smoothed out, his fingers are still, full lips slack.

Only interrupted by his own yawning, Dean deftly unties Jerry's shoes and slips them off, setting them quietly at the foot of his bed so as not to wake him—in all honesty he could probably belt out "That's Amore" at full volume and it wouldn't wake Jerry up, but just in case.

Pulling the sheets up to Jerry's chin, Dean takes one last look at Jerry—hoping that things will be normal tomorrow—and slips out of the room.

Chapter Thirty-Two

**The next morning**

Please be fine. Please be fine. Please be fine. Dean hopes, oh he hopes that the effects of the joint from last night have worn off.

He's wrong. Jerry's fine—except for the fact he finds everything funny. At this point Dean's not even worried about Jerry anymore—really—he's just wondering what the hell they're going to do about the show they've got to do tonight!

Jerry, who looks fine, and is all dressed and ready for the day, is loud enough that Dick, whose room is across from theirs, comes shuffling in with a bewildered expression.

"He's still goin', this kid?" Dick asks Dean, setting Jerry off into a fit of giggles. Again.

"For Pete's sake, is there *anything* we can give him to settle down?" Dean asks, knowing that Dick is the most experienced with this kind of thing, which is hard to believe given his track record.

"Hair of the dog."

"What?" Dean fixes Dick with a confused, slightly annoyed gaze.

"Trust me, Dino. This'll fix him up right away. It balances the high." With that said, Dick retrieves another joint from his breast pocket and Dean strikes a match for him to light it. Finally he gives it to Jerry, whose nose crinkles at the acrid stench. "Okay, Jer. Nice and easy. Just one or two small puffs, and you'll feel like a new man."

Dean and Dick watch breathlessly for some miraculous turn of behavior, but they are disappointed. Back to square one. No, square negative seventeen. A minute later Jerry's just as

*The Crooner and The Comic*

bad as he was last night in the limo.

"I can't WAIT to go to rehearsal and tell everyone I tried pot! Isn't that cool?" Jerry gazes at them with an exuberant smile and flushed cheeks.

Paling, Dean says with a serious tone to make sure Jerry understands explicitly, "You can't say that to anyone. It's against the law." Jerry doesn't give Dean any indications he really understands what was just said, and blinks as if he can't really see clearly. Dread turning his stomach, Dean grips Jerry by the shoulder. "Jer, are you going to be all right? I don't want to let you go on stage and humiliate yourself."

Trying to be serious, Jerry takes a deep breath and chews on his lower lip in contemplation.

"I'll be okay, Paul, really." Like hell he'll be.

\*\*\*

Jerry is honestly surprised he was able to slog through rehearsals, with how heavy his limbs feel, and how . . . foggy his mind is. Everything feels like it takes ten seconds longer to do. Including think.

"Take a walk with me, Jer." Turning around to face Dean, Jerry's eyes widen. Although he's high, he still knows how weird it is Dean's asking him this. He doesn't walk unless he has to. What would he do without golf carts?

"Okay." Jerry says in a small voice, and follows him out into the great courtyard of the campus, and the bitingly winter air. The ground, as far as the eye can see, is a glimmering white—the snow from last night's storm hasn't melted yet, and boy are Jerry's eyes suffering for it. It feels like someone's pressing on his eyes with a hot poker and going all the way

## Chapter Thirty-Two

through his head.

"Listen, Jer . . . You gotta understand that this isn't the same as drinking too much . . . " Dean begins, patiently explaining what Jerry needs to know about the joint he smoked. Although he struggles to keep up with what Dean is saying, finding his attention easily diverted by things he sees on the way, Jerry feels a swell of pride. He can't help thinking how many things Dean knows, and how . . . wise he is. And how he's got Dean.

Finally they come to a stop, and fixing Jerry with a searching gaze, Dean says, "Look, Jer. If you don't feel like you can make it tonight, I'll cancel the whole gig." Jerry thinks about his aching legs, and the pounding headache, but then thinks about the 3,000 people who have already bought tickets, and how far they drove to come here.

"Not on your life!"

\* \* \*

As Jerry falls back onto his bed that night, gratefully succumbing to sleep, he half-wishes he had let Dean talk him out of performing. He started off well, and ended well, but he knows the middle will haunt his dreams forever (what was he thinking! How did talking about college somehow transition to an awkward sex talk!).

# Chapter Thirty-Three

Names: Dean Martin and Jerry Lewis

Year: 1952

Ages: 35 and 26

Finally this is Jerry's chance. His last prank failed miserably when he had replaced Dean's Woodhue with coca-cola and water, and Dean had found out but kept silent about it for days so that Jerry was on edge the entire time just waiting. But now he has the perfect idea.

   The car ride back to the Ambassador Hotel is quiet as both Dean and Jerry sit exhausted from their final show, with the only difference being that Jerry's mind is working like crazy. It's finally the end of their two week stint at the Chicago Theater, where they had been doing *seven shows a day*.

## Chapter Thirty-Three

As tired as he felt, Jerry was shocked nonetheless when just before stepping into the limo from the show Dean had turned to him with heavy-lidded eyes, rubbed his hand over the side of his face, and said, "Jer, I'm outta gas. I'm really very tired." There was something about *Dean* saying that which made Jerry realize he had a right to be legitimately tired.

\* \* \*

Finally they arrive at the hotel, and, needing an excuse to get back into the suite before Dean goes up, Jerry manages to convince him to have a nightcap in the Pump Room. As soon as they order, Jerry says as casually as he can, barely able to hide his smile of glee, that he has to go to the men's room. Dean shrugs, slouched in his seat with legs stretched all the way out under the table, and Jerry hurries into the elevator despite the aching in his legs.

Once Jerry's up in their suite and spots Dean's bed, a thrill of energy runs through him as he begins the process of short-sheeting the bed. It's not very hard to do, and doesn't take Jerry more than three minutes, but it feels like there's some invisible weight pushing down on his arms, and he has to stop and rest every thirty seconds.

Finally he's done and he steps back with a grin. Dean won't suspect a thing.

\* \* \*

Dean's hunched over frame disappears behind the doorway to his part of the suite, and Jerry waits there just outside the door, heart thudding as he awaits Dean's reaction—hopefully

## The Crooner and The Comic

a laugh. Two thumps of Dean's shoes falling at the foot of his bed, the rustling of him pulling back his sheets, and a heavy sigh. No laugh or cry of annoyance.

Jerry strains to hear something, anything else! But silence descends upon the room, and Jerry purses his lips, confused. A moment or two later he decides to risk it all and take a look to see what went wrong.

As soon as he rounds the door, Jerry spots Dean fast asleep, curled up at the corner of the bed with the softest snore escaping his parted lips. He must have been so exhausted he never even noticed!

Jerry shakes his head, disappointed. Maybe next time.

\* \* \*

Names: Dean Martin and Jerry Lewis

Year: 1953

Ages: 36 and 27

"Well, hot diggety. I've never seen so many books 'cept in the library—even then, I've never been inside one!" Dean exclaims with an appreciative whistle, hands shoved in his pockets as he looks back to Marilyn and Jerry from the living room wall

## Chapter Thirty-Three

that is in fact a bookshelf.

"I just like to read, that's all." Marilyn says quietly, lips curving upwards as she gazes at the ground shyly. Dean and Jerry exchange a knowing glance, and then Jerry exaggeratedly flings himself onto the long white couch and says with jaw jutting forward, "Anyone got any drinks around here?"

With the softest of laughs, Marilyn looks up at Jerry stretched out on the couch and goes into the other room to get them drinks. Still at the bookshelf, Dean traces a row of books with a finger until he settles on a wide-spined red one whose title Jerry can't see from there, and plucks it out of the row.

Jerry then watches in curious amusement as Dean crosses the room in two long strides and sits down on the far end of the couch with legs crossed, cracking open the book and leafing through the pages with a contemplative expression. Jerry knows full well Dean doesn't read. Period. Save comic books, at least, and so it takes Jerry every ounce of self restraint not to call him out on it, because at the end of the day he knows Dean's lack of formal education is a bit of a sore spot.

When Marilyn comes back in, she seems slightly surprised, but also secretly pleased, as she hands Dean a martini on the rocks, and ends up sitting between us with her legs curled up underneath her.

"You're beautiful, you know that?" Dean abruptly says, but upon noting the torn expression that crosses her face, adds almost without pause, "You must be tired from everyone saying that to you." She doesn't say anything, but just kind of gazes out the window towards the backyard, a distant expression in her clear eyes.

Before either of the two can say anything else, Marilyn says with a strong voice, "They're always saying how lucky I am. How pretty I am, and how much money I have. What a nice house I have."

"But . . . ?" Jerry asks, for Marilyn had said all of that with an odd disdain, still staring out of the window with wide eyes.

"I don't mean to sound . . . ungrateful, but I don't want it. Any of it. It's no use, I never even get to go places I want and see people—" Marilyn's voice that has gotten softer and softer is cut off by Dean standing up and helping her stand as well. Jerry just watches, a little stunned, as Dean leans in to whisper something into Marilyn's ear. Immediately the haunted expression leaves Marilyn's face, and she breaks into a toothy smile, murmuring something back to Dean before leaving the room.

After buttoning his jacket and straightening his collar with hands that seem too large for his body, Dean nimbly retrieves a cigarette and pinches it between two fingers.

"Light?" He turns to Jerry, as if nothing had happened, and Jerry just squints at him and fires back, "What the hell was that all about?"

"Oh, nothing. Mar's just tired. She's gonna get some shuteye." Dean takes out a match himself and lights his cigarette before sitting down in the chair across from Jerry. An odd feeling washes over Jerry as he stares at the almost . . . bored expression on Dean's face.

"No, seriously, Paul, what the hell was she talking about?"

"You're thinking too much about things, Jer. She was just tired. She's been kinda stressed out lately with all her work, that's all. Now, do you want Chinese or burgers? We can stop by that great new place on 34th street on the way back to the hotel." Dean's already getting up and putting on his overcoat,

## Chapter Thirty-Three

puffing lazily on the cigarette between his teeth.

   A cold feeling washes over Jerry, and he frowns, not sure why he feels like something's off with the whole situation. He could have sworn Marilyn was saying things that weren't normal . . . like she was unhappy, but Dean seemed *so* sure. Dean wouldn't have any reason to lie to him.

# Chapter Thirty-Four

Names: Dean Martin and Jerry Lewis

Year: 1953

Ages: 36 and 27

"What are you doing?" Dean tries to sound casual, and succeeds—he doesn't sound like he cares what Jerry's response is, actually.
 "Darning a sock." Comes his reply through the phone, and Dean just sits there, breathing out smoke through his nose. Waiting until the Kid remembers he's already told him that joke. "Why, what's up?"
 "Wanna take a ride?" Dean asks, barely able to conceal the pride in his voice.
 "Ooh, goody, I love rides." Jerry exclaims, sliding into his

## Chapter Thirty-Four

Idiot voice, and then out of it the next instant: "Where we going?"

"It's a surprise. See you outside." Hanging up the phone, Dean crushes his cigarette in the nearest ashtray and bounds out of his trailer, taking a moment to admire the new, glinting blue paint on his Cadillac convertible parked just a few feet away before hopping behind the wheel.

A minute later Jerry appears from his dressing room, and when he catches sight of Dean in his car, grinning like a madman, he shakes his head, but smiles nonetheless. As soon as Jerry slides in beside him, Dean starts the engine. Sweet music to his ears.

As they get the okay to pull through the studio gates, Dean grins. A break from running lines for the next scene or sitting around waiting to sing to some broad. Time to relax. They pass a few tourists who have stopped to stare at the pillared arch of the studio, all of whom point and stare with eyes just about to fall out of their heads. What a kick.

As they ride down Sunset Boulevard, warm air tugging at their hair, Jerry holds his arm out the window and closes his eyes, feeling the warmth of the summer sun on his eyelids, and smiles. He doesn't have to look around to know that they're attracting a lot of attention—simply because of the car. And he loves it.

A sideways glance to Dean tells Jerry he loves it, too. The warm crinkling at the corners of his eyes, the grin that tugs at the corner of his lips as he smokes his Camel. What's not to love?

Dean finally stops the car and Jerry glances up to see the blue, circular sign titled "Music City", and his eyes drop to the tall store window, in which is a huge picture of Dean to

*The Crooner and The Comic*

proclaim the arrival of his new single, "That's Amore."

Resting one arm behind Jerry's headrest, Dean points with the other and says gleefully, "Hey, is that a handsome Italian, or what?"

*\*\*\**

Names: Dean Martin and Jerry Lewis

Year: 1953

Ages: 36 and 27

"Is this an endurance contest? When can I get some *real* food?" Dean complains as soon as Jerry enters the hospital room, eyes flashing with the anger of one truly starving. It's only been a few days since he got an operation for his hernia.

"I'll go to Lindy's and get you some nice chicken soup. That'll be good for you" Jerry answers immediately, springing on the opportunity to do something for Dean. Somehow he still hasn't managed to forget what he did a month ago. How stupid! The very thought of it makes him shudder in embarrassment. He really thought that it would be a good idea to learn golf so he could play with Dean. Wrong! It ended up just being him taking yet another thing that Dean alone is good at where he doesn't have to be around all the chaos.

So that Dean wouldn't be able to argue, Jerry ducks out of the room and passes the elevators to sprint down the stairs. He

## Chapter Thirty-Four

had made the mistake of heading up here in the elevator, and had to go up the entire time listening to a wheelchair-ridden older man struggling for breath. Images flashed through his mind of his grandmother on a stretcher being taken out of the house, mouth unable to form words, glassy eyes helpless.

Finally Jerry makes it out of the hospital and flags down a cab in record time.

"Where to?"

"Take me to Lindy's at Fifty-first Street and Broadway, and step on it!" Jerry gives the driver kudos for trying to step on it, but God just doesn't seem to be on his side this time, for as they cross 121st street, out of nowhere they're hit with a thunderstorm. Lightning, thunder, rain pouring like its gushing from the ocean, the whole shebang.

It seems like they're moving less than a mile an hour, and Jerry finds himself checking his watch every thirty seconds, which, surprisingly, doesn't speed anyone up.

Finally, an *hour* later, they're at Lindy's, and five minutes later Jerry's back out in the rain, holding a very hot cup of soup in a paper bag, doing his best to shield it from getting wet. It takes him only a second to realize that he made a mistake. A soon to be very costly mistake. There's no taxi available, so, with heart sinking to the pit of his stomach in despair, Jerry begins the long walk back to the hospital.

He just thinks about how happy Dean will be to see that he did all of that for him, and how proud he'll be. But it's hard to hold onto those images when *right now* your clothes are soaked through, and you can feel the heat being sucked from the soup as each block goes by. Jerry's legs are starting to ache, and each new gust of wind sends him into an episode of shivering so hard he's sure his bones are rattling inside.

## The Crooner and The Comic

Jerry doesn't even know how many minutes—or hours, for that matter—have passed when he sees he's on Broadway and 112th Street. At the thought of having to go another twenty-five blocks, he feels like giving up right then and there, but he just wants to see the look on Dean's face—he's convinced himself somehow that Dean needs him, because that's a little less shameful.

Suddenly he starts hearing this flapping—or smacking, rather— against the pavement every time he takes a step. It doesn't take Jerry long to realize the next unfortunate incident that has befallen him is that half the sole of his shoe has come unglued. Damnit. Not only does he have to very probably get hypothermia, but now he's gotta be annoyed to death?

\* \* \*

Finally...*finally* he's in the hospital, too tired to even feel the stares of those around him, his only mission to get to Dean's room. To his astonishment, Dean isn't the worried mess he thought he'd be, he's sitting in bed, watching some John Wayne movie with a Lucky in his mouth.

With numb fingers Jerry strips the soaked paper bag from the jar he can hardly believe was ever piping-hot, and displays the soup with a triumphant smile. Dean just glances over at him, taking in his . . . wet state, and says with a completely straight face, "No matzo balls?"

# Chapter Thirty-Five

Names: Dean Martin and Jerry Lewis

Year: 1953

Ages: 36 and 27

Heart pumping to the same wild tempo of the audience's applause, Jerry steps up to the microphone, staring out victoriously at the crowd. He's done it. He's really performed at the Palladium. His dad would be so proud. His chest tightens for a moment when he thinks about that, but then pushes it aside to begin his ending speech.

"When we return—" Jerry's cut off midsentence by a distant but clear voice shouting, "Never come again!" Astonishment renders him momentarily speechless.

"Go home, Martin and Lewis!" The second shout is followed

by complete chaos: the crowd erupts into simultaneous cheers and boos, sending Jerry's mind into a panic. Are they booing him and Dean? Why did they not want them to come back?

As the curtains cascade down towards the stage, Jerry catches Dean's eye, and sees those same questions echoing through his partner's mind.

\* \* \*

The answer was simple: bad politics, Jack Keller had told them the day after the performance. Anti-American sentiments ever since the end of WWII. Most of the crowd was booing the people who had shouted in the first place. But try explaining that to the press!

Scum. Parasites. Those are just a few of the words Dean used to describe the British press as the event appeared on the front page of every major newspaper.

**MARTIN & LEWIS BOOED AT PALLADIUM OPENING**

Those headlines may not have been accurate, but the people didn't know that—nor did they care. Less and less people showed up to their remaining performances at the Palladium. A difficult thing, sure, but at the end of the day it was how Dean and Jerry would respond that would decide how bad things would get.

\* \* \*

Dean sits upright on his bed, surrounded by several of the newspapers that had come out about the incident. The more he looks at them, the more aware he is of the rage pulsing

## Chapter Thirty-Five

through his veins. Who the hell do these people think they are? They're supposed to be reporting the truth, and this is a far cry from the truth.

Taking out a cigarette, Dean pinches it between his lips as he tries to spark his lighter. Click. Nothing. Click. Nothing. With a frustrated sigh, Dean crushes his cigarette in the ashtray and hurls his lighter against the wall. It doesn't leave a damn mark.

Fuming, Dean picks up the paper closest to him and tears it in half. He doesn't stop to think about why he's angry. He tells himself it's the slander. He tells himself they have no right to do this to him. He quickly pushes away the thought of how good it feels to finally be able to be angry about what they say about him. Really angry.

* * *

Jerry feels a lump form in the back of his throat. He knows what the papers say isn't true. He knows he and Dean did a good job—a great job, for heaven's sake! But still . . . other people might not know that. They might think they did a bad job. But what does he care about what they think? He doesn't know why, but he does care.

Swallowing his frustration, Jerry lights a cigarette. He can't let this get to him; not when Dean is *so* angry. He's gotta help him. Honestly, as much as Jerry wants to be as angry as Dean, he's a little bit shocked. This isn't like Dean at all, and he doesn't like this side of him.

He remembers back a few weeks ago when Keller was telling them about what really happened, and showing them the papers for the first time. Sure, Jerry had his own issues with

## The Crooner and The Comic

the press hitting them below the belt like that, but it really unnerved him when he heard Dean exclaim, "We did the best show of our lives, and they run headlines like that!"

It wasn't exactly *what* he said—although that was odd, since Dean usually is the one to ignore those sorts of things— it was the way he said it. His face was twisted in anger, eyes blazing, and the words came out through clenched teeth. Jerry had felt like a kid who fell off his bike, and was looking up to his dad, searching for that comforting tone and soft caress, only to find eyes wide in panic and lips pressed tightly together.

The phone ringing pulls Jerry from his thoughts, and he reluctantly answers it. It's Keller. He's been trying to get in touch with Jerry for days. Jerry had been fine with no communication about work; it's called vacation for a reason.

"We've really got a problem here." Problem? What new problem could they possibly have? Oh. Dean.

Immediately after Keller hangs up, Jerry worriedly dials Dean's phone in L.A., chewing on the inside of his cheek.

"Hi, pallie." Dean's tone confirms everything Keller just told Jerry.

"Dean, please let it go. You're making this a very tough situation for us—" Jerry begins, but Dean cuts him off, his voice low and his words quick as he says, "Listen, pal, I've just begun."

"Come on, Paul, this isn't worth it."

"These scumbags can't get away with this shit! They're gonna be sorry they didn't go after Cohn and Schine instead of Martin and Lewis!" Dean's voice rises in uncharacteristic anger, and Jerry frowns, wondering. Wondering what to do to clean up Dean's mess. Wondering how to get Dean to see clearly. Wondering why this is making Dean so damn mad.

## Chapter Thirty-Five

\*\*\*

Names: Dean Martin and Jerry Lewis

Year: 1954

Ages: 37 and 28

"Jerry?" Marilyn's voice is soft, distant, like she's not really talking to him.
"Yeah?" He glances away from the pool and to her beside him—she's wearing rolled up jeans and a white button up shirt, and he thinks it looks just beautiful on her. What wouldn't? She's gazing at him searchingly now, and says, a little stronger, "You're not dumb or . . . ugly."
"Thanks?" At the puzzled look on his face, Marilyn giggles softly, and adds, "No, that's not what I mean, it's just that, well, you make everyone think you are dumb and ugly, but you're not. You're not really the guy who makes funny faces and such. But you do it because you think that's what everyone else wants you to do."
Jerry glances away, cheeks burning. Those crystal eyes are too probing, too revealing. He looks down to the pool beneath his feet. The rippling surface is just splashes of ocean blue and lime green on which specks of light and shadow from the trees around them dance across. How does she know? Moreover, how can she blame him for that? Who wants to see the real Jerry Lewis? The Jerry Lewis who has opinions about everything. The Jerry Lewis who has worries about

everything. The Jerry Lewis who's not so funny, and not so cool.

## Chapter Thirty-Six

Names: Dean Martin and Jerry Lewis

Year: 1954

Ages: 37 and 28

It's a wonder Jerry's watch isn't broken. He must have pulled it out a hundred times in the last hour. But it didn't make time move any slower. It certainly didn't make Dean show up to the set.

Finally Jerry spots the glint of the sun against greased, black curls, and that familiar . . . frown. What's Dean thinking, coming an hour late? He knows how Wallis gets when there are delays in production.

He keeps striding towards Jerry; the epitome of casual indifference to his being late. Jerry just stands there, rooted to

## The Crooner and The Comic

the ground, waiting to see what Dean is going to say to him. A crew member passes by Dean, and he gets a joke and a wide smile that Jerry himself hasn't received in weeks. Maybe more. Jerry is hopeful, biting his lip anxiously as Dean comes toward him as if in slow motion. Finally Dean's eyes flit to Jerry's, and recognition darkens them. Dean's face shifts into a mask of distaste that makes Jerry's blood run cold, and he stops.

"Anytime you wanna call it quits, let me know." Such malice. Jerry tries to push away the panic and fear, choosing the joking route: "But, Paul, what would I do without you?"

"Screw yourself, for starters." Another withering look, and Dean's gone.

Jerry's throat constricts, and for a moment he thinks he might be sick. He can't articulate the whys or hows; doesn't want to, but he knows what he feels. He'd be able to smell it a mile away: fear. Fear that courses through his veins like acid and seeps into his very bones.

\* \* \*

Names: Dean Martin and Jerry Lewis

Year: 1954

Ages: 37 and 28

Why can't Jerry just leave things be? Why does he have to try to be like Charlie freakin' Chaplain? He doesn't have to be better than everyone else.

## Chapter Thirty-Six

Dean exhales loudly and presses the palm of his hands against his closed eyes until he can see sparkles. Three knocks on the door elicits a groan, but Dean drops his hands and strides across the room to answer it.

When the door swings open, for the fraction of a second Dean considers shutting it in Jerry's face. But he decides not to. He doesn't have to stay and talk; he forgot that he was getting ready to go out golfing. Forcing his mouth to move, Dean says in a polite tone, "Look, Jer, I'm headed out to the country club."

The corner of Jerry's mouth twitches, and he squints in concentration before mumbling, "We really have to talk, Paul." Although just half a minute ago Dean was ready to rip Jerry's head off, now he's just . . . deflated.

"Why don't you ride out with me."

\* \* \*

"I know there's less in this role than you deserve. I believe in you, Paul. I believe you could carry a movie all by yourself if you wanted." Jerry sounds sincere over the soft rumbling of the car engine, and Dean hates him for it. He's glad they're in the car, because it gives him an excuse to not have to look Jerry in the eye.

Sure, Dean's heard that a million times before, but where does flattery stop and truth begin? He can sing. But for a whole movie? Even singing on stage for a whole hour has got to get tiresome for an audience. As for Sinatra? He's a whole 'nother kind of cat.

"Well—" Dean pauses. If Jerry really thinks that, why is he always trying to take over the movie? Because he could carry a movie by himself, too. "I don't know 'bout that."

## The Crooner and The Comic

"Well, I do." Jerry responds without hesitation, "I'm absolutely sure of it. And I want to tell you something else. I know you're not a hundred percent with the direction we've been going in lately." That's one way to put it. "I understand that, and I understand why. It's a tricky place we're in now—I'm growing, you're growing. Who knows where it'll all end up. But I think we can still have some fun, Paul. I want you to try and remember how good it can be when we're enjoying ourselves. Just give me this one movie, and I'll try like hell to get back to the good times."

Dean blinks, surprised at the memories that flood his mind, like they were just lying in wait for the perfect moment to appear. Clouds that look like they're on fire as the sun peeks above the ocean horizon after a long night of shows. The warm California sun on his cheeks and cool wind through his hair as they drive down Sunset. The look of joy—more joy than he had thought possible— on the Kid's face when he complimented him.

The anger gone, for now, Dean sticks out a big hand, and Jerry takes it.

## Chapter Thirty-Seven

Names: Dean Martin and Jerry Lewis

Year: 1955

Ages: 37 and 29

Heart thrumming with excitement, Jerry approaches Dean's dressing room door. He's gonna be able to go back to Brown's Hotel! He's gonna get to see Charlie again, who never let him down. Who always knew when Jerry needed a comforting word or silent arm around the shoulder. And Lily, and *Lonnie* . . . Jerry smiles at the thought of her. Although he doesn't want to admit it to himself, there's no use in hiding the fact that he's going to be able to return triumphant. He's no longer the busboy or the failed athletic director. He's not the same scrawny, lonely kid who needed their charity. He's got the

## The Crooner and The Comic

world in the palm of his hand now, a partner, a wife, and two beautiful boys.

He makes his presence known and lets himself in. Dean's laying on his couch, head tipped back as he blows smoke through his nostrils.

"Guess what, Paul! You'll never believe it, but we just got this amazing deal to appear at a gala premiere at Brown's Hotel—the one I used to work at— and they're paying for everything. Oh, and they're naming their theater after us!" Jerry bursts out, eager for Dean's eyes to light up, for him to sit up and tell him how excited he is. But that's just the foolish dreaming of a kid.

Dean sits up alright, but there's no hint of excitement in his dark eyes as he says without emotion, "You should have consulted me first." Jerry's heart drops like a stone, and he swallows the lump that forms in his throat as it occurs to him Dean may not go because he didn't ask him.

"I'm consulting you now," Jerry forces himself to say back, just as indifferent as Dean. "Give me the word and we'll do it. If not, we won't."

A pause. A long, slow, breath. Then, words that make Jerry sigh in relief: "Actually, Jerry, I really don't care where we hold it." Jerry's just too relieved that he doesn't stop to think another second about Dean's coldness towards him. Or about the fact that Dean may not have meant yes after all.

*** 

Three knocks on Jerry's office door bring him reluctantly from his directorial edit of next week's big scene.

"Come in."

## Chapter Thirty-Seven

"Hi, Jerry. I don't mean to bother you or nothin', but . . . " It's Maxie, and as he comes in he doesn't seem to know what to do with himself, looking around the room and folding and unfolding his arms.

When nothing else is said, Jerry sighs and looks up from his papers. "Mack, do ya have something to say? You're making me nervous just standing there."

"Your partner isn't making the trip." Jerry's heart skips a beat.

"Are you putting me on?"

A sad grimace and, "Look, Jerry, I'm relaying this straight from Dean's mouth. He said he's tired. He's going to take Jeanne on a trip to Hawaii. What else can I tell you?"

"Alright, Mack." Is all Jerry trusts himself to say, for he feels the heat rising to his cheeks, and he stands up swiftly from his desk to face the window away from Mack.

Mack stands there for a few more moments before he gets the message, and just says a soft, "I *am* sorry, Jerry," before leaving the room. How could this happen? Dean said he was going to go . . . Jerry pinches the bridge of his nose in frustration. No he didn't. Now what is he going to do? He's gonna have to show up there alone. Alone in front of Charlie, and Lillian, and Lonnie . . . and the rest of the newspeople who are going to be there. For a moment Jerry considers feigning a migraine or some other phantom illness. No. That would be worse than showing up alone.

\* \* \*

*The Crooner and The Comic*

Names: Dean Martin And Jerry Lewis

Year: 1955

Ages: 38 and 29

Jerry's stomach twists as he hangs up the phone. Did he really just do the same thing that got him into so much trouble just four months ago? He wasn't really doing anything wrong, right? After all, if Dean was here on the call, he wouldn't have said no to the benefit. That would have been suicide given all the shit Y. Frank got them both out of. Right?
 Unlike last time, Jerry enters Dean's dressing room warily, and apologetically. Dean says nothing when he opens the door, but his look says it all: affection, suspicion, caution—probably rightly so.
 "Hey, pal. I hate to okay this without your approval, but something important has come up."
 "Is it a contract?"
 "Sort of." Jerry bites his lip. He wishes he had asked Dean to come onto the call, too. It wouldn't have been a hassle for Y. Frank, he's sure of it.
 "Okay, then sign it. You'll do it anyhow." Dean says disinterestedly, crossing the room to go back to the Western he was watching.
 "No, this is a little different . . . Y. Frank needs our help at the poor-children's benefit on November the tenth." Jerry watches Dean's face in agonizing anticipation, and Dean doesn't even look his way as he responds, "Sure, he's got it." Remembering last time, Jerry sits down beside Dean and says slowly and

## Chapter Thirty-Seven

carefully, "Dean, hold on, now. This doesn't involve money or contracts. This is Y. Frank, the guy who kept our cars from getting repossessed. Do you understand what I'm saying?" The guy who saved both their hides in pure, unadulterated trust.

"Hey, man—I told you. It's okay." A hint of annoyance creeps into Dean's voice as he tries to talk to Jerry and watch the TV at the same time. The ultimate move of indifference.

"Well, I'm gonna ask you to do something for me, so I can rest easy. I want you to stick your big grubby Italian paw in mine and agree that you'll do the benefit for Y. Frank."

With an exasperated sigh, Dean shakes his hand—probably just so he can go on watching his Western—and says, "Jerry, for Pete's sake, I know how important this is. You got it."

### November 11-The Day of the Benefit

He stood Jerry up. That *meshugener* really stood him up. This was their reputations on the line; Y. Frank's trust on the line.

With steam practically rolling out of Jerry's ears, he walks right into Dean's dressing room without so much as a knock.

"You crossed me, Paul."

"What are you talking about?" This *shit-heel*.

"I'm talking about your *handshake*. You gave me your word that we'd do Y. Frank's benefit." Jerry can barely keep his voice from trembling in fury as he glares at Dean.

"You're out of your mind. I don't know a thing about it." Dean gazes up at him with a look of feigned innocence.

"Where were you last night?"

"When did my life become your business?" Dean fires back mercilessly, and Jerry finds himself blinking back tears in spite of himself. When did Dean's life *stop* being Jerry's business? It seems like just yesterday they were closer than brothers: touring the world together, sleeping in the same room together, sharing makeup, sharing towels . . . sharing life. Together both.

"I didn't mean it that way. I mean, I sent notes to your dressing room, your wife, your valet, and your country club. So you mean to tell me you didn't know you were supposed to be at the Shrine at eight o'clock last night?"

No twitch of the lip. No fast blinking. No break in the voice. Just a cool, indifferent lie as Dean says, "Nobody told me there was going to be a benefit." What? How can Jerry even respond to that? Is this really how it is between them now? Is it *possible* Dean's telling the truth?

While Jerry's staring forward glassy-eyed, Dean's rummaging through his desk for something to write on. He then jots down a note on the back of a typed sheet of paper, and, as if he's talking to his assistant, says cheerily, "Listen, Jer. I need two prints of *Living it Up*. Could you handle that for me?"

Snapping from his trance, Jerry takes the note and excuses himself. Once Dean's door is shut behind him, he looks at both sides of the note. It's the memo for the benefit he had given to Dean.

Fear, anger, and confusion fill Jerry as he stares down at the paper. Is he losing his partner?

## Chapter Thirty-Eight

Names: Dean Martin and Jerry Lewis

Year: 1956

Ages: 38 and 30

"I don't think you should do the scene this way. It's just not funny!" Jerry exclaims, waving the script that's in his hand for everyone to see. Frank Tashlin runs a hand over his mouth and squints at Jerry for a moment before shouting out, "STOP! EVERYONE STOP WHAT THEY'RE DOING! COME OVER HERE!"

From camera man to errand boy, everyone obeys and circles around Frank and Jerry with bewildered glances and muted whispers. "I want you off the set."

"You what?" Jerry says indignantly, masking his panic with

outrage.

"I mean it, Jerry. Off! You're a discourteous, obnoxious prick—an embarrassment to me and a disgrace to the profession." Every word feels like a blow to the stomach, and Jerry tries to ignore the astonished stares of the crew that bring back memories he didn't even know he had.

"Hey, Tish, whoa—calm down. When did you get the right—" He's interrupted quickly and coldly by Frank, "Jerry, as director of this picture, I order you to leave. Go. Get your ass out of here and don't come back."

\* \* \*

Kicked off the set. Jerry was actually kicked off the set. His cheeks burn as he recalls the stares and the murmurs behind his back as he had to leave in shame. For some reason he recalls third grade. Being held back, and having the new kids file in one by one. He remembers the dejection he felt. The embarrassment.

As he lays on his couch in the dark of the den, gazing up at the ceiling through blurred vision, he feels like Joey Levitch again.

He must be so naive for thinking he'd never have to feel the sting of rejection again; being a nobody again. What was he doing? Jerry doesn't *want* to be an obnoxious prick. He doesn't *want* everyone to hate him—he might just die if everyone hates him . . . So, what's wrong with him? Jerry knows, but he doesn't want to even think it, because then it's real. Then it's true.

His eyes sting as tears rise, and he pounds a fist against the couch in frustration. The worst part of it all is that Dean

## Chapter Thirty-Eight

probably won't bat an eyelash—he'll probably be happy about it, now that Jerry's come to think of it.

\* \* \*

Please pick up. Oh, Tish, please…"Yes, what is it?" After more than five failed calls, Tish's exasperated voice is music to Jerry's ears.

"Tish, I'm sorry. I can't tell you how sorry I am. I was wrong. All I ask is, please, let me come back." Jerry says with choked words, trying to push back his pride just this once. There's a terrible silence on the other end, and then, "Will you behave?"

"Gosh, yes! I'll keep my trap shut like my life depends on it!" It kinda does.

"Okay. Report to work in the morning. The shoot is at seven o'clock." Jerry thinks he's never been happier.

"I'll be there at six. And Tish . . . thanks."

"For what?"

"I don't know, maybe for saving my life."

\* \* \*

*The Crooner and The Comic*

Names: Dean Martin and Jerry Lewis

Year: 1956

Ages: 38 and 30

Crinkling of plastic. Slow, heavy footsteps approaching. Finally a voice Jerry recognizes even through the muddle of drugs and pain: "Jerry I've come to see you." Dad? Jerry wants to respond, tries to respond, but his mouth won't form words at first. He cracks open his eyes and takes a moment to focus on his dad standing over him.
 His dad's head is tilted, eyes narrowed darkly with a slight frown tugging down on his lips. "What happened to you?" Jerry's heart drops.
 "Not a thing." He somehow manages, meeting that unfeeling gaze through misty eyes. "I'm taking a vacation . . ."
 His dad leans in closer, glaring at him. Then: "Do you know what you're doing to your mother?" Jerry wants to cry. He wants to do anything rather than be here. His eyes drift closed—hoping to succumb to sleep. He doesn't know why he keeps hoping for something different every time. It's not naivete. It's not compassion or forgiveness. It's just pure stupidity.

*  *  *

A stress-induced arrhythmia. These past ten days, Jerry hasn't stopped marvelling at how close he had been to death. That could've been a heart attack. He almost died. All because of

## Chapter Thirty-Eight

the way Dean's treating him; Jerry can't take it anymore.

Jerry swallows and fumbles with his tie. It's time to confront the inevitable, or he might just literally die. Finally he catches sight of Dean across the lot, and his breath hitches in his throat as he forces himself to walk right up to Dean.

"I've got to talk to you."

"Talk." Dean mutters impatiently. That's all?

Jerry begins, "Well, I think it's a hell of a thing . . . all I can think of is that what we do is not very important. Any two guys could have done it. But even the best of them wouldn't have had what made us as big as we are."

"Yeah? What's that?"

Jerry's heart quickens, and he says in a small voice, hoping: "Well, I think it's the love that we had—that we still have— for each other."

Dean glances down at his shoes. Hating what Jerry has just done. Hating what Jerry is forcing him to say. Hating himself for what he has to say.

Dean looks into Jerry's eyes; bright emerald eyes lit by the afternoon sun . . . full of hope, full of fear . . . a child's eyes.

"You can talk about love all you want," Dean begins with a voice purposely distant. He knows what he must say. He knows that this is the only option left for him—for them. So why can't the Kid see it? How can he still gaze at Dean with those hopeful eyes? How can he hope to fix something that's so broken? The edges aren't just chipped and worn—can't he see the pieces just can't fit back together? But no . . . he can't. That's why Dean has to break his heart. Take his hope. Make him leave, because Dean's no good for him. Look what he's about to do! After all the gifts, all the tears, all the *love* Jerry's given him—more love surely than Dean thought possible for another man to give—he's going to say this lie . . . "To me, you're nothing but a f***ing dollar sign."

# Chapter Thirty-Nine

Names: Dean Martin and Jerry Lewis

Year: 1956

Ages: 39 and 30

"Ladies and Gentlemen, the Copacabana presents . . . Martin and Lewis!" The crowd goes ballistic, and one would have thought it was Ike himself coming out onto the stage. But no, it's just the broken-hearted Monkey and the Organ Grinder who refuses to break face—he would hold that mask over the scars beneath even if it killed him.

 The act is seamless—a little too perfect—the usual fraternal glint in Dean's eyes is missing as he chastises the putz, and Jerry's smile trembles slightly as the voice in his head shouts above the crowd, "It's over! It's over, and there's nothing you

## The Crooner and The Comic

can do about it!"

Finally their last song of the night comes, and the crowd can sense the turmoil that hangs in the air as the fated words are sung, "You and me, we're gonna be pardners." But the 'pardners' can taste it. They can feel it deep in their bones. That's why Dean looks out to the crowd in disdain as they shout and plead for the two to stay together as if they're in pain. As if they have any idea what it feels like to be torn apart from the inside out.

The last line comes, and Jerry wishes more than anything—like a kid on his birthday, eyes squeezed shut as he blows out his candles—that the line can last forever so it doesn't have to be over; really over.

"You and me will be the greatest pardners, buddies and pals." The words come out wrong in his mouth, a little strangled over the lump that forms in Jerry's throat, and he shoots a sideways glance towards Dean, as if seeing his partner distraught—just this once—would make everything better. But he has to swallow his disappointment as Dean just smiles towards the audience, unwilling to let anyone in, least of all Jerry.

No. No, it doesn't mean anything. Jerry refuses to let himself believe that Dean truly meant it—that Jerry's nothing more than a dollar sign to him. How can Dean not love him when Jerry loves Dean so much?

The two bow deeply, staring out at the crowd through blurred vision, and they stumble off the stage together as if it's on fire.

Somehow Jerry ends up in his own room, flopped on the bed like a kid who's just been yelled at by his parents. His cheeks already shine with tears; he has no reason to conceal them—if

## Chapter Thirty-Nine

anything they are a proud virtue—a mark of true love. A wave of nausea rolls over him as he realizes he has no idea what he's going to do for the rest of his life, and he wishes he *could* be sick. He wishes he could get all of the feelings out of him as easy as that.

It would be better to feel nothing at all than to feel this broken—this empty. His eyes flutter closed wearily, lashes thick with tears, and he feels himself falling, tumbling over and over in space like a feather—down into a trackless desert . . . *No sign of life anywhere. Not a solitary bird crosses the sky. Even the stars are gone. I struggle forward, engulfed in a wide river of sand.*

*Suddenly the desert spreads open. A highway shimmers before me. I'm walking on it—to where? Then the movie marquee!—It straddles the highway; ornate, gilded, the lights flashing round and round.*

*There, appearing in bulging, silvery brightness is the most enormous word I have ever seen:*
### ALONE

*I stagger, sink to my knees. I'm screaming at the top of my lungs:*
"ONE! ONE! ONE ALONE!"

Jerry holds a cigarette to his mouth with trembling fingers, and it takes a few tries to get it between his lips. He takes a deep drag and presses the base of his palms to his closed eyes until he can see sparkles. He can do it. He has to.

He drops his hands and looks down at the phone with trepidation as he moves to tell the operator to connect him with Dean. He just talked to Patti, and she and the kids were going to meet him at the airport. At least he had her.

## The Crooner and The Comic

She understood his hurt. She was going to make him feel better—for a little while.

"Hello, pallie, how're ya holdin' up?" That smooth, relaxed voice makes Jerry press the phone to his forehead, fighting the urge to scream, or cry—or both.

"I don't know yet. I just want to say . . . we've had some good times, Paul." There's a hint of hope in his voice, waiting for some miraculous turn of heart.

"There'll be more."

"Yeah . . . well . . . take care of yourself, that's all—"

"You too, pardner." This could be their last conversation, and Dean couldn't stay on the line a blasted five minutes?

"I love you." Jerry breathes, praying his partner says it back. He didn't even have to really mean it. Jerry would believe him no matter what.

"I love you, too."

The click of the line disconnecting widens Jerry's bloodshot eyes as he realizes what this means. A surge of desperation wells up inside of him. It would be better to hate Dean than to love him this much. Need him this much. He needs Dean in his life like he needs air. He needs to hear his voice again. He needs to bury his head in Dean's shoulder when he can turn to no one else. He needs to see that smile again and feel perfectly safe and loved and warm inside.

\* \* \*

Dean holds the half-empty glass of whiskey with his thumb and middle finger, turning it slightly so the liquid swishes around in a slow, circular motion. It's like dark honey falling over itself, with the occasional fleck of gold bubbling to the

## Chapter Thirty-Nine

surface. It's like the glimmering he had caught in Jerry's eyes tonight—the hazel darkening in something he didn't quite know—something he didn't want to know.

Goddamnit, it's not like he ever wanted to hurt the kid! Since when was it his fault that the kid needed him? He didn't make Jer's dad an ass! He didn't make Jer's mom a useless, tired excuse for a parent!

Dean abruptly slams his glass down on the table in front of him, the sound jarring him from his thoughts. He pushes them away gladly and into the back of his mind, and hopefully they would stay there forever. He didn't need this. Life has to move on, he has to move on and do things on his own. Friendships like theirs just don't last. The world doesn't let them.

Drip. He glances down, surprised at the tear that splashes onto his thumb. Why was he crying? Last time Dean checked, he wasn't a kid, and he sure as hell wasn't a broad. He's felt it before, though: a tightening in his chest, this burning in his eyes and feeling like he had to take in rapid breaths or he would pass out. But he can always make it go away. He takes a swig of whiskey, a drag with eyes shut tightly, and once he opens them, he's fine. This time he wouldn't be so lucky . . . He can feel the crack in his mask spreading, growing like a cancer until everything falls apart.

A shudder runs through his body, and he gasps out, surprised at the pain. Whether he likes it or not, he loves Jer—but how can he? How can he love him when he so hates the Idiot's annoying, nasally voice that cuts into his head all hours of the day; hates his need to control everything; hates how Jerry calls him up in the middle of the night 'cause he can't sleep; hates how he has to have a brand new pack of cigarettes and brand new pair of long white socks everyday . . . But most

## The Crooner and The Comic

of all he hates that haunted, pleading look on Jerry's face that tells him the Kid hurt himself, and he needs Dean to tell him everything's going to be okay, even if it really isn't.

He guesses he does love him. And he hates himself for it.

Ring. Ring. Ring. Dean knows who it is before he even touches the phone. His eyes close and he takes in a deep breath before picking it up.

"Hello, pallie, how're ya holdin' up?"

"I don't know yet. I just want to say…we've had some good times, Paul." Jer's voice is somewhat restrained and hoarse, like he's been crying—which Dean knows he has—and although he doesn't want to, he imagines the Kid holding himself on his bed, lips too close to the mouthpiece, fingers tangled in the wire.

"There'll be more." Dean finds himself saying, and it makes him sick. He knows it's a lie, but a lie's better than nothing. It's better than having to endure the silence broken only by the Kid's sniffing back a sob.

"Yeah . . . well . . . take care of yourself, that's all—" The fact that Jerry's not shouting at him to take him back or trying to be funny makes Dean feel that much worse, and he interrupts, "You too, pardner."

"I love you." Dean's mind races, and his mouth goes dry. He wants to lie, knows he can come up with one in a split second, but this time he won't.

"I love you, too."

# Chapter Forty

Names: Dean Martin and Jerry Lewis

Year: 1976

Ages: 59 and 50

Why does Jerry feel like *something's* going to happen? It seems to him like Frank has been acting strangely around him. Sure, it could be the exhaustion of having to stand on this stage for hours on end- there's no way the telethons were always this hard. It could be the pounding headache barely dimmed by a couple Percodans popped just before the show. But still, Jerry just has a feeling that something is going to happen…

Frank's voice echoing across the stage and through the room jolts him from his thoughts: "Listen, I have a friend who loves what you do every year, and who just wanted to come out and

## The Crooner and The Comic

say hi- would you send my friend out, please? Wh-where is he?" As Jerry watches Frank turn towards the right wing of the stage, voice calm and expression the epitome of casual, a spotlight follows his gaze and illuminates this mystery guest. Oh God. Jerry's heart drops into the pit of his stomach, and suddenly all he can see is Dean lazily strutting towards him with a wonderful, warm smile on his sun-kissed face that Jerry thinks is just as handsome as it was twenty years ago. Jerry's not sure whether he's happy out of his skull or nauseous, and he hands his microphone to a grinning Frank- the bastard- and is surprised to find his hands are trembling.

Finally Dean has reached him, and all the fear and anxiety swirling within him evaporates as Jerry wraps his arms around Dean in a full embrace. It's like nothing has changed as Jerry buries his face in Dean's shoulder, and almost feels like crying at the fact that he can't go back to when things were good between them, and they were living life together. He feels a sort of desperation well up inside of him.

He thinks Dean must feel the same because Dean's hand comes up to his shoulder and grips him tightly by the lapel. Desperately. Finally they have to let go, and Dean kisses him on the cheek. So easily. Like they only saw each other a day ago. Jerry reaches up to cup Dean's cheek. Just to look at him a little longer. He hadn't realized just how much he missed Dean until now.

"Alright, alright, break it up! What is this here?!" Frank playfully pushes them apart, and Jerry swallows his disappointment. The moment was over. He forces himself to chuckle, but can't help wringing his hands. It's the only way to stop himself from shaking. *Like a warm cup of coffee and a beautiful sunset, it comforts for a moment, then disappears forever. Here I*

## Chapter Forty

am, Jerry Lewis. Alone in a crowd.

# Afterword

In the process of writing this book, I've come to see God more clearly through the relationship of Dean and Jerry. In one sense I now see God in every aspect of creation. On the one hand I see the creation as an image and a reflection of the greater creator. On the other hand, I see the broken world around me, and God as the solution.

Think of a wonderful, beautiful song played on a violin, and it's just the most amazing song you've ever heard. Do you give your congratulations and heap your praises upon the violin? No, of course not. You look to the one playing the violin. Now imagine the praise you would have if the one playing the violin was also the creator of the violin. Likewise, I see the creation and see how beautiful it is, but attribute the real praise to the one who made them and planned every step in their lives.

Looking at Dean and Jerry's relationship when they were close—closer than brothers—I see reflections of God's love for me: I think of Jerry walking all those blocks in the pouring rain just to bring back Dean a jar of soup; I think of Dean wordlessly protecting Jerry—from himself more often than not. In this relationship part of the beauty was the willing

## Afterword

self—sacrifice for the other person; it's what you see in the best of friendships and the best of marriages. The things Dean and Jerry did for each other point to the greater sacrifice that God made for me—for you—of giving up His perfect son to die so we could be in relationship with God.

In Jerry's honesty I see the beautiful, human vulnerability; his telling those who he loved how much he loved them in almost schmaltzy honesty, and his telling the world shamelessly his fears and foibles. As much as some look down upon this kind of honesty as being feminine, or a weakness, it is a wonderful human attribute that should be celebrated. Honestly and openly telling those we love just how much we love them, even when it makes us vulnerable. And when we all have faults, foibles, and even sins, and confessing them to those affected regardless of our reputation.

In Dean I see courage to make decisions for himself, rather than be held back by perceived obligations to the world. I see so many people just crippled by what others think—even those they don't know! So what results is an inability to take risks and be free. To take it one step further, Dean should not have be constrained by the world's standards and criticques, but in order to bring glory to God! He should have not used his freedom for himself, but to serve others.

Now, not only are there so many beautiful aspects of Dean and Jerry worthy of praise to God, but there are painful sides that show me just how much we need a Savior. For we live in a fallen world, meaning that this is not the way it was intended to be. We were supposed to live in a paradise without sin, without tears, and without pain. But because of our sin, we fell away from God, unable to enjoy perfect relationship and paradise with Him—that is, until He sacrificed His one and only son Jesus for our sins.

For those of you who enter into Dean and Jerry's story, and their relationship, when it fractured, it pains you. Although their split was inevitable because of jealousy, pride, ambition, and fear, it still hurts. Sometimes tremendously. Why? Because we know that's not the way things are supposed to be. Relationships are not supposed to be broken. This is why we need Jesus' transforming love. Once we see what He's done for us, and the freedom that comes in knowing He loves us always and loves us perfectly—despite who we are—then we can leave our old lives of sin and take on the new lives of holiness. He gives you a relationship that can never be broken. Grace is life-changing. With Jesus' love and transforming power, we can overcome sin's grasp and lead wonderful relationships with others. He would be able to soothe Jerry's debilitating fears through his unconditional acceptance and love, and through His promises to always be with us through every storm and moment. He would be able to redirect Jerry's ambition from being for himself to being for God's Kingdom.

Looking at just how much Jerry needed and thirsted for love and acceptance from others, I see how Jesus would have completed him. How only Jesus could offer him unconditional, unmerited love, and would never forsake him when so many others did. "He who did not spare his own Son, but gave him up for us all—how will he not also, along with him, graciously give us all things? " (Romans 8: 32).

With all of this, how are you looking at Dean and Jerry? How do you view the world? Are you seeing the beauty in nature, the people you love, and tasty food as marvelous gifts from the ultimate gift-giver that lead you to worship? If not, how

*Afterword*

are you viewing the world? For even if you do not articulate your view, you still have one. Deep down you are living based on your subconscious view of the world.

When you see the fallen nature of the world, when someone sins against you, or you sin against others, what are you viewing as the solution? Are you looking for self-help books? Or are you looking to Jesus Christ, the Savior of the world?

I hope that Dean and Jerry lead you to the truth of the world around you, and why you exist.

\* \* \*

## Bibliography

Levy, Shawn. *King of Comedy*. St. Martin's Press, 1996. *Amazon Kindle*.

Lewis, Jerry. *The Total Filmmaker*. Random House, 1971.

Lewis, Jerry, and Herb Gluck. *Jerry Lewis: In Person*. Jerry Lewis and Herb Gluck, 1982.

Lewis, Jerry, and James Kaplan. *Dean & Me: A Love Story*. DOUBLEDAY, 2005.

Lewis, Patti, and Sarah A. Coleman. *I Laffed Till I Cried*. Waco, TX, WRS Publishing, 1993.

Tosches, Nick. Living High in the Dirty Business of Dreams. New York, Dell Publishing, 1992.

Printed in Great Britain
by Amazon